JACK HIGGINS

A PRAYER FOR THE DYING

HARPER

Harper
An imprint of HarperCollins*Publishers*
77–85 Fulham Palace Road,
Hammersmith, London W6 8JB

www.harpercollins.co.uk

This paperback edition 2008
1

First published in Great Britain by
William Collins Sons and Co. 1973

Copyright © Jack Higgins 1973

Harry Patterson asserts the moral right to
be identified as the author of this work

A catalogue record for this book is
available from the British Library

ISBN-978-0-00-723488-2

Typeset in Sabon by Palimpsest Book Production Limited,
Grangemouth, Stirlingshire
Printed and bound in Great Britain by
Clays Ltd, St Ives plc

Mixed Sources
Product group from well-managed
forests and other controlled sources
www.fsc.org Cert no. SW-COC-1806
© 1996 Forest Stewardship Council

FSC

FSC is a non-profit international organisation established to promote the
responsible management of the world's forests. Products carrying the FSC
label are independently certified to assure consumers that they come
from forests that are managed to meet the social, economic and
ecological needs of present and future generations.

Find out more about HarperCollins and the environment at
www.harpercollins.co.uk/green

PUBLISHER'S NOTE

A PRAYER FOR THE DYING was first published in the UK by William Collins Sons and Co. in 1973 and in 1996 by Signet, but has been out of print for some years.

In 2008, it seemed to the author and his publishers that it was a pity to leave such a good story languishing on his shelves. So we are delighted to be able to bring back A PRAYER FOR THE DYING for the pleasure of the vast majority of us who never had a chance to read the earlier edition.

For Philip Williams, The Expert

1

Fallon

When the police car turned the corner at the end of the street Fallon stepped into the nearest doorway instinctively and waited for it to pass. He gave it a couple of minutes and then continued on his way, turning up his collar as it started to rain.

He walked on towards the docks keeping to the shadows, his hands pushed deep into the pockets of his dark-blue trenchcoat, a small dark man of five feet four or five who seemed to drift rather than walk.

A ship eased down from the Pool of London sounding its foghorn, strange, haunting – the last of the dinosaurs moving aimlessly through some primeval swamp, alone in a world already alien. It suited his mood perfectly.

There was a warehouse at the end of the street facing out across the river. The sign said *Janos Kristou – Importer*. Fallon opened the little judas gate in the main entrance and stepped inside.

The place was crammed with bales and packing cases of every description. It was very dark, but there was a light at the far end and he moved towards it. A man sat at a trestle table beneath a naked light bulb and wrote laboriously in a large, old-fashioned ledger. He had lost most of his hair and what was left stuck out in a dirty white fringe. He wore an old sheepskin jacket and woollen mittens.

Fallon took a cautious step forward and the old man said without turning round, 'Martin, is that you?'

Fallon moved into the pool of light and paused beside the table. 'Hello, Kristou.'

There was a wooden case on the floor beside him and the top was loose. Fallon raised it and took out a Sterling submachine-gun thick with protective grease.

'Still at it, I see. Who's this for? The Israelis

or the Arabs or have you actually started taking sides?'

Kristou leaned across, took the Sterling from him and dropped it back into the box. 'I didn't make the world the way it is,' he said.

'Maybe not, but you certainly helped it along the way.' Fallon lit a cigarette. 'I heard you wanted to see me.'

Kristou put down his pen and looked up at him speculatively. His face was very old, the parchment-coloured skin seamed with wrinkles, but the blue eyes were alert and intelligent.

He said, 'You don't look too good, Martin.'

'I've never felt better,' Fallon told him. 'Now what about my passport?'

Kristou smiled amiably. 'You look as if you could do with a drink.' He took a bottle and two paper cups from a drawer. 'Irish whiskey – the best. Just to make you feel at home.'

Fallon hesitated and then took one of the cups. Kristou raised the other. 'May you die in Ireland. Isn't that what they say?'

Fallon swallowed the whiskey down and crushed the paper cup in his right hand. 'My passport,' he said softly.

3

Kristou said, 'In a sense it's out of my hands, Martin. I mean to say, you turning out to be so much in demand in certain quarters – that alters things.'

Fallon went round to the other side of the table and stood there for a moment, head bowed, hands thrust deep into the pockets of the blue trenchcoat. And then he looked up very slowly, dark empty eyes burning in the white face.

'If you're trying to put the screw on me, old man, forget it. I gave you everything I had.'

Kristou's heart missed a beat. There was a cold stirring in his bowels. 'God help me, Martin,' he said, 'but with a hood on you'd look like Death himself.'

Fallon stood there, eyes like black glass staring through and beyond and then suddenly, something seemed to go out of him. He turned as if to leave.

Kristou said quickly, 'There is a way.'

Fallon hesitated. 'And what would that be?'

'Your passport, a berth on a cargo boat

leaving Hull for Australia, Sunday night.' He paused. 'And two thousand pounds in your pocket to give you a fresh start.'

Fallon said incredulously, 'What do I have to do? Kill somebody?'

'Exactly,' the old man answered.

Fallon laughed softly. 'You get better all the time, Kristou. You really do.'

He reached for the whiskey bottle, emptied Kristou's cup on the floor and filled it again. The old man watched him, waiting. Rain tapped against a window as if somebody was trying to get in. Fallon walked across and peered down into the empty street.

A car was parked in the entrance to an alley on his left. No lights – which was inter-esting. The foghorn sounded again, farther downriver this time.

'A dirty night for it.' He turned. 'But that's appropriate.'

'For what, Martin?' Kristou asked.

'Oh, for people like you and me.'

He emptied the cup at a swallow, walked

back to the table and put it down in front of Kristou very carefully.

'All right,' he said, 'I'm listening.'

Kristou smiled. 'Now you're being sensible.' He opened a manilla folder, took out a photo and pushed it across the table. 'Take a look at that.'

Fallon picked it up and held it under the light. It had obviously been taken in a cemetery and in the foreground there was a rather curious monument. A bronze figure of a woman in the act of rising from a chair as if to go through the door which stood partly open between marble pillars behind her. A man in a dark overcoat, head bare, knelt before her on one knee.

'Now this.' Kristou pushed another photo across.

The scene was the same except for one important fact. The man in the dark overcoat was now standing, facing the camera, hat in hand. He was massively built, at least six foot two or three, with chest and shoulders to match. He had a strong Slav face with high flat cheekbones and narrow eyes.

'He looks like a good man to keep away from,' Fallon said.

'A lot of people would agree with you.'

'Who is he?'

'His name's Krasko – Jan Krasko.'

'Polish?'

'Originally – but that was a long time ago. He's been here since before the war.'

'And where's here?'

'Up North. You'll be told where at the right time.'

'And the woman in the chair?'

'His mother.' Kristou reached for the photo and looked at it himself. 'Every Thursday morning without fail, wet or fine, there he is with his bunch of flowers. They were very close.'

He put the photos back in the manilla folder and looked up at Fallon again. 'Well?'

'What's he done to deserve me?'

'A matter of business, that's all. What you might call a conflict of interests. My client's tried being reasonable, only Krasko won't play. So he'll have to go; and as publicly as possible.'

'To encourage the others?'

'Something like that.'

Fallon moved back to the window and looked down into the street. The car was still there in the alley. He spoke without turning round.

'And just what exactly is Krasko's line of business?'

'You name it,' Kristou said. 'Clubs, gambling, betting shops . . .'

'Whores and drugs?' Fallon turned round. 'And your client?'

Kristou raised a hand defensively. 'Now you're going too far, Martin. Now you're being unreasonable.'

'Good night, Kristou.' Fallon turned and started to walk away.

'All right, all right,' Kristou called, something close to panic in his voice. 'You win.'

As Fallon moved back to the table, Kristou opened a drawer and rummaged inside. He took out another folder, opened it and produced a bundle of newspaper clippings. He sorted through them, finally found what he was looking for and passed it to Fallon.

The clipping was already yellowing at the edges and was dated eighteen months previously. The article was headed *The English Al Capone*.

There was a photo of a large, heavily-built man coming down a flight of steps. He had a fleshy, arrogant face under a Homburg hat and wore a dark-blue, double-breasted melton overcoat, a handkerchief in the breast pocket. The youth at his shoulder was perhaps seventeen or eighteen and wore a similar coat, but he was bare-headed, an albino, with white shoulder-length hair that gave him the look of some decadent angel.

Underneath the photo it said; *Jack Meehan and his brother Billy leaving Manchester Central Police Headquarters after questioning in connection with the death of Agnes Drew.*

'And who was this Agnes Drew?' Fallon demanded.

'Some whore who got kicked to death in an alley. An occupational hazard. You know how it is?'

'I can imagine.' Fallon glanced at the photo

9

again. 'They look like a couple of bloody undertakers.'

Kristou laughed until the tears came to his eyes. 'That's really very funny, you know that? That's exactly what Mr Meehan is. He runs one of the biggest funeral concerns in the north of England.'

'What, no clubs, no gambling? No whores, no drugs?' Fallon put the clipping down on the table. 'That's not what it says here.'

'All right,' Kristou leaned back, took off his spectacles and cleaned them with a soiled handkerchief. 'What if I told you Mr Meehan is strictly legitimate these days? That people like Krasko are leaning on him. Leaning hard – and the law won't help.'

'Oh, I see it all now,' Fallon said. 'You mean give a dog a bad name?'

'That's it.' Kristou slammed a fist against the table. 'That's it exactly.' He adjusted his spectacles again and peered up at Fallon eagerly. 'It's a deal then?'

'Like hell it is,' Fallon said coldly. 'I wouldn't touch either Krasko or your friend Meehan with a bargepole. I might catch something.'

'For God's sake, Martin, what's one more on the list to you?' Kristou cried as he turned to go. 'How many did you kill over there? Thirty-two? Thirty-four? Four soldiers in Londonderry alone.'

He got up quickly, his chair going backwards, darted round the table and grabbed Fallon by the arm.

Fallon pushed him away. 'Anything I did, I did for the cause. Because I believed it was necessary.'

'Very noble,' Kristou said. 'And the kids in that school bus you blew to a bloody pulp. Was that for your cause?'

He was back across the table, a hand of iron at his throat, staring up into the muzzle of a Browning automatic and behind it Fallon and the white devil's face on him. There was the click of the hammer being cocked.

Kristou almost fainted. He had a partial bowel movement, the stench foul in the cold, sharp air of the warehouse and Fallon pushed him away in disgust.

'Never again, Kristou,' he whispered and the Browning in his left hand was rock-steady.

11

'Never again.' The Browning disappeared into the right-hand pocket of his trenchcoat. He turned and walked away, his footsteps echoing on the concrete floor. The Judas gate banged.

Kristou got up gingerly, tears of rage and shame in his eyes. Someone laughed and a harsh, aggressive Yorkshire voice said from the shadows, 'Now that's what I call really being in the shit, Kristou.'

Jack Meehan walked into the light, his brother Billy at his heels. They were both dressed exactly as they had been in the newspaper photo. It really was quite remarkable.

Meehan picked up the clipping. 'What in the hell did you want to show him that for? I sued the bastard who wrote that article and won.'

'That's right.' Billy Meehan giggled. 'The judge would have made it a farthing damages only there's no such coin any more.' His voice was high-pitched, repellent – nothing masculine about it at all.

Meehan slapped him casually, back-handed across the mouth, and said to Kristou, his

12

nose wrinkling in disgust, 'Go and wipe your backside, for Christ's sake. Then we talk.'

When Kristou returned, Meehan was sitting at the table pouring whiskey into a clean paper cup, his brother standing behind him. He sampled a little, spat it out and made a face. 'All right, I know the Irish still have one foot in the bog, but how can they drink this muck?'

'I'm sorry, Mr Meehan,' Kristou said.

'You'll be a bloody sight sorrier before I'm through with you. You cocked it up proper, didn't you?'

Kristou moistened dry lips and fingered his spectacles. 'I didn't think he'd react that way.'

'What in the hell did you expect? He's a nutcase, isn't he? I mean, they all are over there, going round shooting women and blowing up kids. That's civilised?'

Kristou couldn't think of a thing to say, but was saved by Billy who said carelessly, 'He didn't look much to me. Little half-pint runt. Without that shooter in his fist he'd be nothing.'

Meehan sighed heavily. 'You know there are days when I really despair of you, Billy.

You've just seen hell on wheels and didn't recognise it.' He laughed harshly again. 'You'll never come closer, Kristou. He was mad at you, you old bastard. Mad enough to kill and yet that shooter didn't even waver.'

Kristou winced. 'I know, Mr Meehan. I miscalculated. I shouldn't have mentioned those kids.'

'Then what are you going to do about it?'

Kristou glanced at Billy, then back to his brother, frowning slightly. 'You mean you still want him, Mr Meehan?'

'Doesn't everybody?'

'That's true enough.'

He laughed nervously and Meehan stood up and patted him on the face. 'You fix it, Kristou, like a good lad. You know where I'm staying. If I haven't heard by midnight, I'll send Fat Albert to see you and you wouldn't like that, would you?'

He walked into the darkness followed by his brother and Kristou stood there, terrified, listening to them go. The judas gate opened and Meehan's voice called, 'Kristou?'

'Yes, Mr Meehan.'

'Don't forget to have a bath when you get home. You stink like my Aunt Mary's midden.'

The judas banged shut and Kristou sank down into the chair, fingers tapping nervously. God damn Fallon. It would serve him right if he turned him in.

And then it hit him like a bolt from the blue. The perfect solution and so beautifully simple.

He picked up the telephone, dialled Scotland Yard and asked to be put through to the Special Branch.

It was raining quite heavily now and Jack Meehan paused to turn up his collar before crossing the street.

Billy said, 'I still don't get it. Why is it so important you get Fallon?'

'Number one, with a shooter in his hand he's the best there is,' Meehan said. 'Number two, everybody wants him. The Special Branch, Military Intelligence – even his old mates in the IRA which means – number three – that he's eminently disposable afterwards.'

'What's that mean?' Billy said as they turned the corner of the alley and moved towards the car.

'Why don't you try reading a few books, for Christ's sake?' Meehan demanded. 'All you ever seem to think of is birds.'

They were at the front of the car by now, a Bentley Continental, and Meehan grabbed Billy by the arm and pulled him up quickly.

'Here, what the hell's going on? Where's Fred?'

'A slight concussion, Mr Meehan. Nothing much. He's sleeping it off in the rear seat.'

A match flared in a nearby doorway pulling Fallon's face out of the darkness. There was a cigarette between his lips. He lit it, then flicked the match into the gutter.

Meehan opened the door of the Bentley and switched on the lights. 'What are you after?' he said calmly.

'I just wanted to see you in the flesh, so to speak, that's all,' Fallon said. 'Good night to you.'

He started to move away and Meehan grabbed his arm. 'You know, I like you, Fallon. I think we've got a lot in common.'

'I doubt that.'

Meehan ignored him. 'I've been reading this German philosopher lately. You wouldn't know him. He says that for authentic living what is necessary is the resolute confrontation of death. Would you agree with that?'

'Heidegger,' Fallon said. 'Interesting you should go for him. He was Himmler's bible.'

He turned away again and Meehan moved quickly in front of him. 'Heidegger?' he said. 'You've read Heidegger?' There was genuine astonishment in his voice. 'I'll double up on the original offer and find you regular work. Now I can't say fairer than that, can I?'

'Good night, Mr Meehan,' Fallon said and melted into the darkness.

'What a man,' Meehan said. 'What a hard-nosed bastard. Why, he's beautiful, Billy, even if he is a fucking Mick.' He turned. 'Come on, let's get back to the Savoy. You drive and if you put as much as a scratch on this motor I'll have your balls.'

Fallon had a room in a lodging-house in Hanger Street in Stepney just off the Commercial Road. A couple of miles, no more, so he walked, in spite of the rain. He hadn't the slightest idea what would happen now. Kristou had been his one, his only hope. He was finished, it was as simple as that. He could run, but how far?

As he neared his destination, he took out his wallet and checked the contents. Four pounds and a little silver and he was already two weeks behind with his rent. He went into a cheap wine shop for some cigarettes then crossed the road to Hanger Street.

The newspaper man on the corner had deserted his usual pitch to shelter in a doorway from the driving rain. He was little more than a bundle of rags, an old London-Irishman, totally blind in one eye and only partially sighted in the other.

Fallon dropped a coin in his hand and took

a paper. 'Good night to you, Michael,' he said.

The old man rolled one milky white eye towards him, his hand fumbling for change in the bag which hung about his neck.

'Is it yourself, Mr Fallon?'

'And who else? You can forget the change.'

The old man grabbed his hand and counted out his change laboriously. 'You had visitors at number thirteen about twenty minutes ago.'

'The law?' Fallon asked softly.

'Nothing in uniform. They went in and didn't come out again. Two cars waiting at the other end of the street – another across the road.'

He counted a final penny into Fallon's hand. Fallon turned and crossed to the telephone-box on the other corner. He dialled the number of the lodging-house and was answered instantly by the old woman who ran the place. He pushed in the coin and spoke.

'Mrs Keegan? It's Daly here. I wonder if you'd mind doing me a favour?'

He knew at once by the second's hesitation, by the strain in her voice, that old Michael's supposition had been correct.

'Oh, yes, Mr Daly.'

'The thing is, I'm expecting a phone call at nine o'clock. Take the number and tell them I'll ring back when I get in. I haven't a hope in hell of getting there now. I ran into a couple of old friends and we're having a few drinks. You know how it is?'

There was another slight pause before she said as if in response to some invisible prompt, 'Sounds nice. Where are you?'

'A pub called The Grenadier Guard in Kensington High Street. I'll have to go now. See you later.'

He replaced the receiver, left the phone-box and moved into a doorway from which he had a good view of No. 13 halfway down the short street.

A moment later, the front door was flung open. There were eight of them. Special Branch from the look of it. The first one on to the pavement waved frantically and two cars moved out of the shadows at the end of the street. The whole crew climbed inside, the cars moved away at speed. A car which was parked at the kerb on the other side of the main road went after them.

Fallon crossed to the corner and paused beside the old newspaper seller. He took out his wallet, extracting the four remaining pound notes and pressed them into his hand.

'God bless you, Mr Fallon,' Michael said, but Fallon was already on the other side of the road, walking rapidly back towards the river.

This time Kristou didn't hear a thing although he had been waiting for something like an hour, nerves taut. He sat there at the table, ledger open, the pen gripped tightly in his mittened hand. There was the softest of footfalls, wind over grass only, then the harsh, deliberate click as the hammer of the Browning was cocked.

Kristou breathed deeply to steady himself. 'What's the point, Martin?' he said. 'What would it get you?'

21

Fallon moved round to the other side of the table, the Browning in his hand. Kristou stood up, leaning on the table to stop from shaking.

'I'm the only friend you've got left now, Martin.'

'You bastard,' Fallon said. 'You sicked the Special Branch on to me.'

'I had to,' Kriston said frantically. 'It was the only way I could get you back here. It was for your own good, Martin. You've been like a dead man walking. I can bring you back to life again. Action and passion, that's what you want. That's what you need.'

Fallon's eyes were like black holes in the white face. He raised the Browning at arm's length, touching the muzzle between Kristou's eyes.

The old man closed them. 'All right, if you want to, go ahead. Get it over with. This is a life, the life I lead? Only remember one thing. Kill me, you kill yourself because there *is* no one else. Not one single person in this world that would do anything other than turn you in or put a bullet in your head.'

There was a long pause. He opened his eyes to see Fallon gently lowering the hammer of the Browning. He stood there holding it against his right thigh, staring into space.

Kristou said carefully, 'After all, what is he to you, this Krasko? A gangster, a murderer. The kind who lives off young girls.' He spat. 'A pig.'

Fallon said. 'Don't try to dress it up. What's the next move?'

'One phone call is all it takes. A car will be here in half an hour. You'll be taken to a farm near Doncaster. An out-of-the-way place. You'll be safe there. You make the hit on Thursday morning at the cemetery like I showed you in the photo. Krasko always leaves his goons at the gate. He doesn't like having them around when he's feeling sentimental.'

'All right,' Fallon said. 'But I do my own organising. That's understood.'

'Of course. Anything you want.' Kristou opened the drawer, took out an envelope and shoved it across. 'There's five hundred quid there in fives, to be going on with.'

23

Fallon weighed the envelope in his hand carefully for a moment, then slipped it into a pocket. 'When do I get the rest?' he said. 'And the passport?'

'Mr Meehan takes care of that end on satisfactory completion.'

Fallon nodded slowly. 'All right, make your phone call.'

Kristou smiled, a mixture of triumph and relief. 'You're doing the wise thing, Martin. Believe me you are.' He hesitated. 'There's just one thing if you don't mind me saying so?'

'And what would that be?'

'The Browning – no good to you for a job like this. You need something nice and quiet.'

Fallon looked down at the Browning, a slight frown on his face. 'Maybe you have a point. What have you got to offer?'

'What would you like?'

Fallon shook his head. 'I've never had a preference for any particular make of handgun. That way you end up with a trademark. Something they can fasten on to and that's bad.'

24

Kristou unlocked a small safe in the corner, opened it and took out a cloth bundle which he unwrapped on the table. It contained a rather ugly-looking automatic, perhaps six inches long, a curious-looking barrel protruding a farther two inches. The bundle also contained a three-inch silencer and two fifty-round cartons of ammunition.

'And what in the hell is this?' Fallon said, picking it up.

'A Czech Ceska,' Kristou told him. 'Seven point five millimetres. Model twenty-seven. The Germans took over the factory during the war. This is one of theirs. You can tell by the special barrel modification. Made that way to take a silencer.'

'Is it any good?'

'SS Intelligence used them, but judge for yourself.'

He moved into the darkness. A few moments later, a light was turned on at the far end of the building and Fallon saw that there was a target down there of a type much used by the army. A lifesize replica of a charging soldier.

As he screwed the silencer on to the end of the barrel, Kristou rejoined him. 'Any time you're ready.'

Fallon took careful aim with both hands, there was a dull thud that outside would not have been audible above three yards. He had fired at the heart and chipped the right arm.

He adjusted the sight and tried again. He was still a couple of inches out. He made a further adjustment. This time he was dead on target.

Kristou said, 'Didn't I tell you?'

Fallon nodded. 'Ugly, but deadly, Kristou, just like you and me. Did I ever tell you that I once saw a sign on a wall in Derry that said: Is there a life before death? Isn't that the funnlest thing you ever heard?'

Kristou stared at him, aghast, and Fallon turned, his arm swung up, he fired twice without apparently taking aim and shot out the target's eyes.

2

Father da Costa

. . . the Lord is my Shepherd, I shall not want.
Father Michael da Costa spoke out bravely
as he led the way up through the cemetery,
his words almost drowned in the rush of
heavy rain.

Inside, he was sick at heart. It had rained
heavily all night, was raining even harder
now. The procession from chapel to graveside was a wretched affair at the best of times,
but this occasion was particularly distressing.

For one thing, there were so few of them.
The two men from the funeral directors
carrying the pitifully small coffin between
them and the mother, already on the point of
collapse, staggering along behind supported
by her husband on one side and her brother

on the other. They were poor people. They had no one. They turned inward in their grief.

Mr O'Brien, the cemetery superintendent, was waiting at the graveside, an umbrella over his head against the rain. There was a gravedigger with him who pulled off the canvas cover as they arrived. Not that it had done any good for there was at least two feet of water in the bottom.

O'Brien tried to hold the umbrella over the priest, but Father da Costa waved it away. Instead, he took off his coat and handed it to the superintendent and stood there in the rain at the graveside, the old red and gold cope making a brave show in the grey morning.

O'Brien had to act as server and Father da Costa sprinkled the coffin with holy water and incense and as he prayed, he noticed that the father was glaring across at him wildly like some trapped animal behind bars, the fingers of his right hand clenching and unclenching convulsively. He was a big man – almost as big as da Costa. Foreman on a building site.

Da Costa looked away hurriedly and prayed for the child, face upturned, rain beading his tangled grey beard.

Into your hands, O Lord,
We humbly commend our sister,
Lead her for whom you have
Shown so great a love,
Into the joy of the heavenly
paradise.

Not for the first time, the banality of what he was saying struck him. How could he explain to any mother on this earth that God needed her eight-year-old daughter so badly that it had been necessary for her to choke to death in the stinking waters of an industrial canal to drift for ten days before being found.

The coffin descended with a splash and the gravedigger quickly pulled the canvas sheet back in place. Father da Costa said a final prayer, then moved round to the woman who was now crying bitterly.

He put a hand on her shoulder. 'Mrs Dalton – if there's anything I can do.'

The father struck his arm away wildly. 'You leave her alone!' he cried. 'She's suffered enough. You and your bloody prayers. What good's that? I had to identify her, did you know that? A piece of rotting flesh that was my daughter after ten days in the canal. What kind of a God is it that could do that to a child?'

O'Brien moved forward quickly, but Father da Costa put up an arm to hold him back. 'Leave it,' he said calmly.

A strange, hunted look appeared on Dalton's face as if he suddenly realised the enormity of his offence. He put an arm about his wife's shoulders and he and her brother hurried her away. The two funeral men went after them.

O'Brien helped da Costa on with his coat. 'I'm sorry about that, Father. A bad business.'

'He has a point, poor devil,' da Costa said, 'After all, what am I supposed to say to someone in his position?'

The gravedigger looked shocked, but O'Brien simply nodded slowly. 'It's a funny old life sometimes.' He opened his umbrella. 'I'll walk you back to the chapel, Father.'

Da Costa shook his head. 'I'll take the long way round if you don't mind. I could do with the exercise. I'll borrow the umbrella if I may.'

'Certainly, Father.'

O'Brien gave it to him and da Costa walked away through the wilderness of marble monuments and tombstones.

The gravedigger said, 'That was a hell of an admission for a priest to make.'

O'Brien lit a cigarette. 'Ah, but then da Costa is no ordinary priest. Joe Devlin, the sacristan at St Anne's, told me all about him. He was some sort of commando or other during the war. Fought with Tito and the Jugoslav partisans. Afterwards, he went to the English College in Rome. Had a brilliant career there – could have been anything. Instead, he decided to go into mission work after he was ordained.'

'Where did they send him?'

'Korea. The Chinese had him for nearly five years. Afterwards they gave him some administrative job in Rome to recuperate, but he didn't like that. Got them to send him to Mozambique. I think it was his grandfather who was Portuguese. Anyway, he speaks the language.'

'What happened there?'

'Oh, he was deported. The Portuguese authorities accused him of having too much sympathy with rebels.'

'So what's he doing here?'

'Parish priest at Holy Name.'

'That pile of rubble?' the gravedigger said incredulously. 'Why, it's only standing up because of the scaffolding. If he gets a dozen for Mass on a Sunday he'll be lucky.'

'Exactly,' O'Brien said.

'Oh, I get it.' The gravedigger nodded sagely. 'It's their way of slapping his wrist.'

'He's a good man,' O'Brien said. 'Too good to be wasted.'

He was suddenly tired of the conversation and, for some strange reason, unutterably depressed. 'Better get that grave filled in.'

'What, now, in this rain?' The gravedigger looked at him bewildered. 'It can wait till later, can't it?'

'No, it damn well can't.'

O'Brien turned on heel and walked away and the grave-digger, swearing softly, pulled back the canvas sheet and got to work.

Father da Costa usually enjoyed a walk in the rain. It gave him a safe, enclosed feeling. Some psychological thing harking back to childhood, he supposed. But not now. Now, he felt restless and ill at case. Still disturbed by what had happened at the graveside.

He paused to break a personal vow by lighting a cigarette, awkwardly because of the umbrella in his left hand. He had recently reduced his consumption to five a day, and those he smoked only during the evening, a pleasure to be savoured by anticipation, but under the circumstances . . .

He moved on into the oldest part of the cemetery, a section he had discovered with delight only a month or two previously. Here amongst the pines and the cypresses were superb Victorian-Gothic tombs, winged angels in marble, bronzed effigies of Death.

33

Something different on every hand and on each slab a pious, sentimental, implacable belief in the hereafter was recorded.

He didn't see a living soul until he went round a corner between rhododendron bushes and paused abruptly. The path divided some ten yards in front of him and at the intersection stood a rather interesting grave. A door between marble pillars, partially open. In front of it the bronze figure of a woman in the act of rising from a chair.

A man in a dark overcoat, head bare, knelt before her on one knee. It was very quiet – only the rushing of the rain into wet earth and Father da Costa hesitated for a moment, unwilling to intrude on such a moment of personal grief.

And then an extraordinary thing happened. A priest stepped in through the eternity door at the back of the grave. A youngish man who wore a dark clerical raincoat over his cassock and a black hat.

What took place then was like something out of a nightmare, frozen in time, no reality to it at all. As the man in the dark overcoat glanced up, the priest produced an automatic with a long black silencer on the end. There was a dull thud as he fired. Fragments of bone and brain sprayed out from the rear of his victim's skull as he was slammed back against the gravel.

Father da Costa gave a hoarse cry, already seconds too late, 'For God's sake no!'

The young priest, in the act of stepping towards his victim, looked up, aware of da Costa for the first time. The arm swung instantly as he took deliberate aim and da Costa looked at Death, at the white devil's face on him, the dark, dark eyes.

And then, unaccountably, as his lips moved in prayer, the gun was lowered. The priest bent down to pick something up. The dark eyes stared into his for a second longer and then he slipped back through the door and was gone.

Father da Costa threw the umbrella to one side and dropped to his knees beside the man who had been shot. Blood trickled from the nostrils, the eyes were half-closed and yet, incredibly, there was still the sound of laboured breathing.

He began to recite in a firm voice, the prayers for the dying. *Go, Christian Soul, from this world, in the Name of God the Father Almighty who created thee* and then, with a hoarse rattle, the breathing stopped abruptly.

Fallon followed the path at the north end of the cemetery, walking fast, but not too fast. Not that it mattered. He was well screened by rhododendron bushes and it was unlikely that there would be anyone about in such weather.

The priest had been unfortunate. One of those time and chance things. It occurred to him, with something like amusement and not for the first time in his life, that no matter how well you planned, something unexpected always seemed to turn up.

He moved into a small wood and found the van parked in the track out of sight as he had left it. There was no one in the driver's seat and he frowned.

'Varley, where are you?' he called softly.

A small man in a raincoat and cloth cap

came blundering through the trees, mouth gaping, clutching a pair of binoculars in one hand. He learned against the side of the van, fighting for breath.

Fallon shook him roughly by the shoulder. 'Where in the hell have you been?'

'I was watching,' Varley gasped. He raised the binoculars. 'Mr Meehan's orders. That priest. He saw you. Why didn't you give it to him?'

Fallon opened the van door and shoved him in behind the wheel. 'Shut up and get driving!'

He went round to the rear, opened the doors, got in and closed them again as the engine roared into life and they lurched away along the rough track.

He opened the small window at the rear of the driver's compartment. 'Steady,' he said. 'Easy does it. The slower the better. A friend of mine once robbed a bank and made his escape in an ice-cream van that couldn't do more than twenty miles an hour. They expect you to move like hell after a killing so do the other thing.'

He started to divest himself of the rain-coat and cassock. Underneath he wore a dark sweater and grey slacks. His navy blue trench-coat was ready on the seat and he pulled it on. Then he took off the rubber galoshes he was wearing.

Varley was sweating as they turned into the dual carriageway. 'Oh, God,' he moaned. 'Mr Meehan will have our balls for this.'

'Let me worry about Meehan.' Fallon bundled the priest's clothing into a canvas holdall and zipped it shut.

'You don't know him, Mr Fallon,' Varley said. 'He's the devil himself when he's mad. There was a fella called Gregson a month or two back. Professional gambler. Bent as a corkscrew. He took one of Mr Meehan's clubs for five grand. When the boys brought him in, Mr Meehan nailed his hands to a table top. Did it himself, too. Six-inch nails and a five-pound hammer. Left him like that for five hours. To consider the error of his ways, that's what he said.'

'What did he do to him after that?' Fallon asked.

38

'I was there when they took the nails out. It was horrible. Gregson was in a terrible state. And Mr Meehan, he pats him on the cheek and tells him to be a good boy in future. Then he gives him a tenner and sends him to see this Paki doctor he uses.' Varley shuddered. 'I tell you, Mr Fallon, he's no man to cross.'

'He certainly seems to have his own special way of winning friends and influencing people,' Fallon said. 'The priest back there? Do you know him?'

'Father da Costa?' Varley nodded. 'Has a broken-down old church near the centre of the city. Holy Name, it's called. He runs the crypt as a kind of doss house for down-and-outs. About the only congregation he gets these days. One of these areas where they've pulled down all the houses.'

'Sounds interesting. Take me there.'

The car swerved violently, so great was Varley's suprise and he had to fight to regain control of the wheel. 'Don't be crazy. My orders were to take you straight back to the farm.'

'I'm changing them,' Fallon said simply and he sat back and lit a cigarette.

The Church of the Holy Name was in Rockingham Street, sandwiched between gleaming new cement and glass office blocks on the one hand and shabby, decaying warehouses on the other. Higher up the street there was a vast brickfield where old Victorian slum houses had been cleared. The bulldozers were already at work digging the foundation for more tower blocks.

Varley parked the van opposite the church and Fallon got out. It was a Victorian-Gothic monstrosity with a squat, ugly tower at its centre, the whole networked with scaffolding although there didn't seem to be any work in progress.

'It isn't exactly a hive of industry,' Fallon said.

'They ran out of money. The way I hear it the bloody place is falling down.' Varley wiped sweat from his brow nervously. 'Let's get out of it, Mr Fallon – please.'

'In a minute.'

Fallon crossed the road to the main entrance. There was the usual board outside with da Costa's name there and the times of Mass. Confession was at one o'clock and five on weekdays. He stood there, staring at the board for a moment and then he smiled slowly, turned and went back to the van.

He leaned in the window. 'This funeral place of Meehan's – where is it?'

'Paul's Square,' Varley said. 'It's only ten minutes from here on the side of the town hall.'

'I've got things to do,' Fallon said. 'Tell Meehan I'll meet him there at two o'clock.'

'For Christ's sake, Mr Fallon,' Varley said frantically. 'You can't do that,' but Fallon was already halfway across the road going back towards the church.

Varley moaned, 'You bastard!' and he moved into gear and drove away.

Fallon didn't go into the church. Instead, he walked up the side street beside a high, greystone wall. There was an old cemetery inside, flat tombstones mainly and a house in one corner, presumably the presbytery. It looked to be in about the same state as the church.

It was a sad, grey sort of place, the leafless trees black with a century of city soot that even the rain could not wash away and he was filled with a curious melancholy. This was what it all came to in the end whichever way you looked at it. Words on cracked stones. A gate clicked behind him and he turned sharply.

A young woman was coming down the path from the presbytery, an old trenchcoat over her shoulders against the rain. She carried an ebony walking stick in one hand and there was a bundle of sheet music under the other arm.

Fallon judged her to be in her late twenties with black shoulder-length hair and a grave, steady face. One of those plain faces that for some strange reason you found yourself looking at twice.

He got ready to explain himself as she approached, but she stared straight through him as if he wasn't there. And then, as she went by, he noticed the occasional tap with the stick against the end of a tomb – familiar friends.

She paused and turned, a slight, uncertain frown on her face. 'Is anyone there?' she called in a calm, pleasant voice.

Fallon didn't move a muscle. She stayed there for a moment longer, then turned and continued along the path. When she reached a small door at the end of the church, she took out a yale key, opened it and went inside.

Fallon went out through the side gate and round to the main entrance. When he pushed open the door and went inside he was conscious of the familiar odour and smiled wryly.

'Incense, candles and the holy water,' he said softly and his fingers dipped in the bowl as he went past in a kind of reflex action.

It had a sort of charm and somewhere in the dim past, some-body had obviously spent a lot of money on it. There was Victorian stained glass and imitation medieval carvings everywhere. Gargoyles, skulls, imagination running riot.

Scaffolding lifted in a spider's web to support the nave at the altar end and it was very dark except for the sanctuary lamp and candles flickering before the Virgin.

The girl was seated at the organ behind the choir stalls. She started to play softly. Just a few tentative chords at first and then, as Fallon started to walk down the centre aisle, she moved into the opening of the Bach Prelude and Fugue in D Major.

And she was good. He stood at the bottom of the steps, listening, then started up. She stopped at once and swung round.

'Is anyone there?'

'I'm sorry if I disturbed you,' he told her. 'I was enjoying listening.'

There was that slight, uncertain smile on her face again. She seemed to be waiting, so he carried on. 'If I might make a suggestion?'

'You play the organ?'

'Used to. Look, that trumpet stop is a reed. Unreliable at the best of times, but in a damp atmosphere like this –' he shrugged. 'It's so badly out of tune it's putting everything else out. I'd leave it in if I were you.'

'Why, thank you,' she said. 'I'll try that.'

She turned back to the organ and Fallon went down the steps to the rear of the church and sat in a pew in the darkest corner he could find.

She played the Prelude and Fugue right through and he sat there, eyes closed, arms folded. And his original judgement still stood. She *was* good – certainly worth listening to.

When she finished after half an hour or so, she gathered up her things and came down the steps. She paused at the bottom and waited, perhaps sensing that he was still there, but he made no sign and after a moment, she went into the sacristy.

And in the darkness at the back of the church, Fallon sat waiting.

3

Miller

Father da Costa was just finishing his second cup of tea in the cemetery superintendent's office when there was a knock at the door and a young police constable came in.

'Sorry to bother you again, Father, but Mr Miller would like a word with you.'

Father da Costa stood up. 'Mr Miller?' he said.

'Detective-Superintendent Miller, sir. He's head of the CID.'

It was still raining heavily when they went outside. The forecourt was crammed with police vehicles and as they walked along the narrow path, there seemed to be police everywhere, moving through the rhododendron bushes.

The body was exactly where he had left it although it was now partially covered with a groundsheet. A man in an overcoat knelt on one knee beside it making some sort of preliminary examination. He was speaking in a low voice into a portable dictaphone and what looked like a doctor's bag was open on the ground beside him.

There were police here everywhere, too, in uniform and out. Several of them were taking careful measurements with tapes. The others were searching the ground area.

The young detective-inspector who had his statement, was called Fitzgerald. He was standing to one side, talking to a tall, thin, rather scholarly-looking man in a belted raincoat. When he saw da Costa, he came across at once.

'There you are, Father. This is Detective-Superintendent Miller.'

Miller shook hands. He had a thin face and patient brown eyes. Just now he looked very tired.

He said, 'A bad business, Father.'

'It is indeed,' da Costa said.

'As you can see, we're going through the usual motions and Professor Lawlor here is making a preliminary report. He'll do an autopsy this afternoon. On the other hand, because of the way it happened you're obviously the key to the whole affair. If I might ask you a few more questions?'

'Anything I can do, of course, but I can assure you that Inspector Fitzgerald was most efficient. I don't think there can be anything he overlooked.'

Fitzgerald looked suitably modest and Miller smiled. 'Father, I've been a policeman for nearly twenty-five years and if I've learned one thing, it's that there's always something and it's usually that something which wins cases.'

Professor Lawlor stood up. 'I've finished here, Nick,' he said. 'You can move him.' He turned to da Costa. 'You said, if I got it right from Fitzgerald, that he was down on his right knee at the edge of the grave.' He walked across. 'About here?'

'That's correct.'

Lawlor turned to Miller. 'It fits, he must

have glanced up at the crucial moment and his head would naturally be turned to the right. The entry wound is about an inch above the outer corner of the left eye.'

'Anything else interesting?' Miller asked.

'Not really. Entry wound a quarter of an inch in diameter. Very little bleeding. No powder marking. No staining. Exterior wound two inches in diameter. Explosive type with disruptions of the table of the skull and lacerations of the right occipital lobe of the brain. The wound is two inches to the right of the exterior occipital protuberance.'

'Thank you, Doctor Kildare,' Miller said.

Professor Lawlor turned to Father da Costa and smiled. 'You see, Father, medicine has its jargon, too, just like the Church. What I'm really trying to say is that he was shot through the skull at close quarters – but not too close.'

He picked up his bag. 'The bullet shouldn't be too far away, or what's left of it,' he said as he walked off.

'Thank you for reminding me,' Miller called ironically.

Fitzgerald had crossed to the doorway and

now he came back, shaking his head. 'They're making a plaster cast of those footprints, but we're wasting our time. He was wearing galoshes. Another thing, we've been over the appropriate area with a tooth comb and there isn't a sign of a cartridge case.'

Miller frowned and turned to da Costa. 'You're certain he was using a silencer?'

'Absolutely.'

'You seem very sure.'

'As a young man I was lieutenant in the Special Air Service, Superintendent,' da Costa told him calmly. 'The Aegean Islands – Jugoslavia. That sort of thing. I'm afraid I had to use a silenced pistol myself on more than one occasion.'

Miller and Fitzgerald glanced at each other in surprise and then Father da Costa saw it all in a flash of blinding light. 'But of course,' he said. 'It's impossible to use a silencer with a revolver. It has to be an automatic pistol which means the cartridge case would have been ejected.' He crossed to the doorway. 'Let me see, the pistol was in his right hand so the cartridge case should be somewhere about here.'

'Exactly,' Miller said. 'Only we can't find it.'

And then da Costa remembered. 'He dropped to one knee and picked something up, just before he left.'

Miller turned to Fitzgerald who looked chagrined. 'Which wasn't in your report.'

'My fault, Superintendent,' da Costa said. 'I didn't tell him. It slipped my mind.'

'As I said, Father, there's always something.' Miller took out a pipe and started to fill it from a worn leather pouch. 'I know one thing. This man's no run-of-the-mill tearaway. He's a professional right down to his fingertips, and that's good.'

'I don't understand,' Father da Costa said.

'Because there aren't many of that calibre about, Father. It's as simple as that. Let me explain. About six months ago somebody got away with nearly a quarter of a million from a local bank. Took all weekend to get into the vault. A beautiful job – too beautiful. You see we knew straight away that there were no more than five or six men in the country capable of that level of craftsmanship and

51

three of them were in jail. The rest was purely a matter of mathematics.'

'I see,' da Costa said.

'Now take my unknown friend. I know a hell of a lot about him already. He's an exceptionally clever man because that priest's disguise was a touch of genius. Most people think in stereotypes. If I ask them if they saw anyone they'll say no. If I press them, they'll remember they saw a postman or – as in this case – a priest. If I ask them what he looked like, we're in trouble because all they can remember is that he looked like a priest – any priest.'

'I saw his face,' da Costa said. 'Quite clearly.'

'I only hope you'll be as certain if you see a photo of him dressed differently.' Miller frowned. 'Yes, he knew what he was doing all right. Galoshes to hide his normal footprints, probably a couple of sizes too large, and a crack shot. Most people couldn't hit a barn door with a handgun at twelve feet. He only needed one shot and that's going some, believe me.'

'And considerable nerve,' Father da Costa

said. 'He didn't forget to pick up that cartridge case, remember, in spite of the fact that I had appeared on the scene.'

'We ought to have you in the Department, Father.' Miller turned to Fitzgerald. 'You carry on here. I'll take Father da Costa down town.'

Da Costa glanced at his watch. It was twelve-fifteen and he said quickly, 'I'm sorry, Superintendent, but that isn't possible. I hear confessions at one o'clock. And my niece was expecting me for lunch at twelve. She'll be worried.'

Miller took it quite well. 'I see. And when will you be free?'

'Officially at one-thirty. It depends, of course.'

'On the number of customers?'

'Exactly.'

Miller nodded good-humouredly. 'All right Father, I'll pick you up at two o'clock. Will that be all right?'

'I should imagine so,' da Costa said.

'I'll walk you to your car.'

The rain had slackened just a little as they went along the path through the rhododendron

53

bushes. Miller yawned several times and rubbed his eyes.

Father da Costa said, 'You look tired, Superintendent.'

'I didn't get much sleep last night. A car salesman on one of the new housing estates cut his wife's throat with a bread knife, then picked up the phone and dialled nine-nine-nine. A nice, straightforward job, but I still had to turn out personally. Murder's important. I was in bed again by nine o'clock and then they rang through about this little lot.'

'You must lead a strange life,' da Costa said. 'What does your wife think about it?'

'She doesn't. She died last year.'

'I'm sorry.'

'I'm not. She had cancer of the bowel,' Miller told him calmly, then frowned slightly. 'Sorry, I know you don't look at things that way in your Church.'

Father da Costa didn't reply to that one because it struck him with startling sudden-ness that in Miller's position, he would have very probably felt the same way.

They reached his car, an old grey Mini van in front of the chapel, and Miller held the door open for him as he got in.

Da Costa leaned out of the window. 'You think you'll get him, Superintendent? You're confident?'

'I'll get him all right, Father,' Miller said grimly. 'I've got to if I'm to get the man I really want – the man behind him. The man who set this job up.'

'I see. And you already know who that is?'

'I'd put my pension on it.'

Father da Costa switched on the ignition and the engine rattled noisily into life. 'One thing still bothers me,' he said.

'What's that, Father?'

'This man you're looking for – the killer. If he's as much a professional as you say, then why didn't he kill me when he had the chance?'

'Exactly,' Miller said. 'Which is why it bothers me too. See you later, Father.'

He stood back as the priest drove away and Fitzgerald appeared round the corner of the chapel.

'Quite a man,' he said.

Miller nodded. 'Find out everything you can about him and I mean everything. I'll expect to hear from you by a quarter to two.' He turned on the astonished Fitzgerald. 'It should be easy enough for you. You're a practising Catholic, aren't you, and a Knight of St Columbia or whatever you call it, or is that just a front for the IRA?'

'It damn well isn't,' Fitzgerald told him indignantly.

'Good. Try the cemetery superintendent first and then there's the Cathedral. They should be able to help. They'll talk to you.'

He put a match to his pipe and Fitzgerald said despairingly, 'But why, for God's sake?'

'Because another thing I've learned after twenty-five years of being a copper is never to take anything or anyone at face value,' Miller told him.

He walked across to his car, climbed in, nodded to the driver and leaned back. By the time they reached the main road, he was already asleep.

4

Confessional

Anna da Costa was playing the piano in the living-room of the old presbytery when Father da Costa entered. She swung round on the piano stool at once and stood up.

'Uncle Michael, you're late. What happened?'

He kissed her cheek and led her to a chair by the window. 'You'll hear soon enough so I might as well tell you now. A man was murdered this morning at the cemetery.'

She gazed up at him blankly, those beautiful, useless, dark eyes fixed on some point beyond, and there was a complete lack of comprehension on her face.

'Murdered? I don't understand.'

He sat down beside her and took both her

hands in his. 'I saw it. Anna. I was the only witness.'

He got up and started to pace up and down the room. 'I was walking through the old part of the cemetery. Remember, I took you there last month?'

He described what had happened in detail, as much for himself as for her, because for some reason it seemed suddenly necessary.

'And he didn't shoot me, Anna!' he said. 'That's the strangest thing of all. I just don't understand it. It doesn't make any kind of sense.'

She shuddered deeply. 'Oh, Uncle Michael, it's a miracle you're here at all.'

She held out her hands and he took them again, conscious of a sudden, overwhelming tenderness. It occurred to him, and not for the first time, that in some ways she was the one creature he truly loved in the whole world, which was a great sin, for a priest's love, after all, should be available to all. But then, she was his dead brother's only child, an orphan since her fifteenth year.

The clock struck one and he patted her head. 'I'll have to go. I'm already late.'

'I made sandwiches,' she said. 'They're in the kitchen.'

'I'll have them when I get back,' he said. 'I won't have much time. I'm being picked up by a detective-superintendent called Miller at two o'clock. He wants me to look through some photos to see if I can recognise the man I saw. If he's early, give him a cup of tea or something.'

The door banged. It was suddenly very quiet. She sat there, thoroughly bewildered by it all, unable to comprehend what he had told her. She was a quiet girl. She knew little of life. Her childhood had been spent in special schools for the blind. After the death of her parents, music college. And then Uncle Michael had returned and for the first time in years, she had somebody to care about again. Who cared about her.

But as always, there was solace in her music and she turned back to the piano, feeling expertly through the Braille music transcripts for the Chopin Prelude she was working on. It wasn't there. She frowned in bewilderment and then suddenly remembered going across to the church earlier to play the organ and the stranger who'd spoken to her. She must have left the piece she wanted over there with her organ transcripts.

She went out into the hall, found a raincoat and a walking stick and let herself out of the front door.

It was still raining hard as Father da Costa hurried through the churchyard and unlocked the small door which led directly into the sacristy. He put on his alb, threw a violet stole over his shoulder and went to hear confession.

He was late – not that it mattered very much. Few people came at that time of day. Perhaps the odd shopper or office worker who found the old church convenient. On some days he waited the statutory half an hour and no one came at all.

The church was cold and smelt of damp, which wasn't particularly surprising as he could no longer meet the heating bill. A young woman was just lighting another candle in front of the Virgin, and as he moved past he was aware of at least two other people sitting waiting by the confessional box.

He went inside, murmured a short prayer and settled himself. The prayer hadn't helped, mainly because his mind was still in a turmoil, obsessed with what he had seen at the cemetery.

The door clicked on the other side of the screen and a woman started to speak. Middle-aged from the sound of her. He hastily forced himself back to reality and listened to what she had to say. It was nothing very much. Sins of omission in the main. Some minor dishonesty concerning a grocery bill. A few petty lies.

The next was a young woman, presumably the one he had seen lighting the candle to the Virgin. She started hesitantly. Trivial matters on the whole. Anger, impure thoughts, lies. And she hadn't been to Mass for three months.

'Is that all?' he prompted her in the silence.

It wasn't, of course, and out it came. An affair with her employer, a married man.

'How long has this been going on?' da Costa asked her.

'For three months, Father.'

The exact period since she had last been to Mass.

'This man has made love to you?'

'Yes, Father.'

'How often?'

'Two or three times a week. At the office. When everyone else has gone home.'

There was a confidence in her voice now, a calmness. Of course bringing things out into the open often made people feel like that, but this was different.

'He has children?'

'Three, Father.' There was a pause. 'What can I do?'

'The answer is so obvious. Must be. Leave this place, find another job. Put him out of your mind.'

'I can't do that.'

'Why?' he said, and added with calculated brutality, 'Because you enjoy it?'

'Yes, Father,' she said simply.

'And you're not prepared to stop?'

'I can't!' For the first time she cracked, just a little, but there was panic there now.

'Then why have you come here?'

'I haven't been to Mass in three months, Father.'

He saw it all then and it was really so beautifully simple, so pitifully human.

'I see,' he said. 'You can't do without God either.'

She started to cry quietly. 'This is a waste of time, Father, because I can't say I won't go with him again when I know damn well my body will betray me every time I see him. God knows that. If I said any different I'd be lying to him as well as you and I couldn't do that.'

How many people were that close to God? Father da Costa was filled with a sense of incredible wonder. He took a deep breath to hold back the lump that rose in his throat and threatened to choke him.

He said in a firm, clear voice, 'May Our Lord Jesus Christ absolve you, and I, by his authority, absolve you from every bond of excommunication and interdict, so far as I can, and you have need. Therefore, I absolve you from your sins in the name of the Father and of the Son and of the Holy Spirit.'

There was silence for a moment and then she said, 'But I can't promise I won't see him again.'

'I'm not asking you to,' da Costa said. 'If you feel you owe me anything, find another job, that's all I ask. We'll leave the rest up to God.'

There was the longest pause of all now and he waited, desperately anxious for the right answer, aware of an unutterable sense of relief when it came. 'Very well, Father, I promise.'

'Good. Evening Mass is at six o'clock. I never get more than fifteen or twenty people. You'll be very welcome.'

The door clicked shut as she went and he sat there feeling suddenly drained. With any luck, he'd said the right thing, handled it the right way. Only time would tell.

It was a change to feel useful again. The door clicked, there was the scrape of the chair being moved on the other side of the grille.

'Please bless me, Father.'

It was an unfamiliar voice. Soft. Irish – an educated man without a doubt.

Father da Costa said, 'May our Lord Jesus bless you and help you to tell your sins.'

There was a pause before the man said, 'Father, are there any circumstances under which what I say to you now could be passed on to anyone else?'

Da Costa straightened in his chair. 'None whatsoever. The secrets of the confessional are inviolate.'

'Good,' the man said. 'Then I'd better get it over with. I killed a man this morning.'

Father da Costa was stunned. 'Killed a man?' he whispered. 'Murdered, you mean?'

'Exactly.'

With a sudden, terrible premonition, da Costa reached forward, trying to peer through the grille. On the other side, a match flared in the darkness and for the second time that day, he looked into the face of Martin Fallon.

* * *

The church was still when Anna da Costa came out of the sacristy and crossed to the choir stalls. The Braille transcripts were where she had left them. She found what she was looking for with no difficulty. She put the rest back on the stand and sat there for a few moments, remembering the stranger with the soft Irish voice.

He'd been right about the trumpet stop. She put out a hand and touched it gently. One thing putting everything else out of joint. How strange. She reached for her walking stick and stood up and somewhere below her in the body of the church, a door banged and her uncle's voice was raised in anger. She froze, standing perfectly still, concealed by the green curtains which hung beside the organ.

Father da Costa erupted from the confessional box, flinging the door wide. She had never heard such anger in his voice before.

'Come out – come out, damn you, and look me in the face if you dare!'

Anna heard the other door in the confessional

box click open, there was the softest of footfalls and then a quiet voice said, 'Here we are
again then, Father.'

Fallon stood beside the box, hands in the
pockets of the navy blue trenchcoat. Father
da Costa moved closer, his voice a hoarse
whisper.

'Are you a Catholic?'

'As ever was, Father.' There was a light
mocking note in Fallon's voice.

'Then you must know that I cannot
possibly grant you absolution in this matter.
You murdered a man in cold blood this
morning. I saw you do it. We both know
that.' He drew himself up. 'What do you want
with me?'

'I've already got it, Father. As you said,
the secrets of the confessional are inviolate.
That makes what I told you privileged
information.'

There was an agony in Father da Costa's
voice that cut into Anna's heart like a knife.
'You used me!' he cried. 'In the worst possible
way. You've used this church.'

'I could have closed your mouth by putting

67

a bullet between your eyes. Would you have preferred that?'

'In some ways I think I would.' Father da Costa had control of himself again now. He said, 'What is your name?'

'Fallon – Martin Fallon.'

'Is that genuine?'

'Names with me are like the Book of the Month. Always changing. I'm not wanted as Fallon. Let's put it that way.'

'I see,' Father da Costa said. 'An interesting choice. I once knew a priest of that name. Do you know what it means in Irish?'

'Of course. Stranger from outside the campfire.'

'And you consider that appropriate?'

'I don't follow you.'

'I mean, is that how you see yourself? As some romantic desperado outside the crowd?'

Fallon showed no emotion whatsoever. 'I'll go now. You won't see me again.'

He turned to leave and Father da Costa caught him by the arm. 'The man who paid you to do what you did this morning, Fallon? Does he know about me?'

68

Fallon stared at him for a long moment, frowning slightly, and then he smiled. 'You've nothing to worry about. It's taken care of.'

'For such a clever man, you really are very foolish,' Father da Costa told him.

The door at the main entrance banged open in the wind. An old woman in a headscarf entered. She dipped her fingers in the holy water, genuflected and came up the aisle.

Father da Costa took Fallon's arm firmly. 'We can't talk here. Come with me.'

At one side of the nave there was an electric cage hoist, obviously used by workmen for access to the tower. He pushed Fallon inside and pressed the button. The cage rose through the network of scaffolding, passing through a hole in the roof.

It finally jerked to a halt and da Costa opened the gate and led the way out on to a catwalk supported by scaffolding that encircled the top of the tower like a ship's bridge.

'What happened here?' Fallon asked.

'We ran out of money,' Father da Costa told him and led the way along the catwalk in the rain.

Neither of them heard the slight whirring of the electric motor as the cage dropped back to the church below. When it reached ground level, Anna da Costa entered, closed the gate and fumbled for the button.

The view of the city from the catwalk was magnificent although the grey curtain of the rain made things hazy in the middle distance. Fallon gazed about him with obvious pleasure. He had changed in some subtle, indefinable way and smiled slightly.

'Now this I like. Earth hath not anything to show more fair: isn't that what the poet said?'

'Great God in heaven, I bring you up here to talk seriously and you quote Wordsworth to me? Doesn't anything touch you at all?'

'Not that I can think of.' Fallon took out a packet of cigarettes. 'Do you use these?'

Father da Costa hesitated, then took one angrily. 'Yes, I will, damn you.'

'That's it Father, enjoy yourself while you can,' Fallon said as he struck a match and gave him a light. 'After all, we're all going to hell the same way.'

'You actually believe that?'

'From what I've seen of life it would seem a reasonable conclusion to me.'

Fallon leaned on the rail, smoking his cigarette, and Father da Costa watched him for a moment, feeling strangely helpless. There was obvious intelligence here – breeding, strength of character – all the qualities and yet it seemed impossible to reach through and touch the man in any way.

'You're not a practising Catholic?' he said at last.

Fallon shook his head. 'Not for a long time.'

'Can I ask why?'

'No,' Fallon told him calmly.

Father da Costa tried again. 'Confession, Fallon, is a Sacrament. A Sacrament of Reconciliation.'

He suddenly felt rather silly, because this was beginning to sound dangerously like one of his Confirmation classes at the local Catholic school, but he pressed on.

'When we go to confession we meet Jesus who takes us to himself and, because we are in him and because we are sorry, God our Father forgives us.'

'I'm not asking for any forgiveness,' Fallon said. 'Not from anybody.'

'No man can damn himself for all eternity in this way,' Father da Costa said sternly. 'He has not the right.'

'Just in case you hadn't heard, the man I shot was called Krasko and he was the original thing from under a stone. Pimp, whoremaster, drug-pusher. You name it, he had a finger in it. And you want me to say sorry? For him?'

'Then he was the law's concern.'

'The law!' Fallon laughed harshly. 'Men like him are above the law. He's been safe for years behind a triple wall of money, corruption and lawyers. By any kind of logic I'd say I've done society a favour.'

'For thirty pieces of silver?'

'Oh, more than that, Father. Much more,' Fallon told him. 'Don't worry, I'll put something in the poor box on the way out. I can afford it.' He flicked his cigarette out into space. 'I'll be going now.'

He turned and Father da Costa grabbed him by the sleeve, pulling him round. 'You're making a mistake, Fallon. I think you'll find that God won't let you have it your way.'

Fallon said coldly, 'Don't be stupid, Father.'

'In fact, he's already taken a hand,' Father da Costa continued. 'Do you think I was there in that cemetery at that particular moment by accident?' He shook his head. 'Oh, no, Fallon. You took one life, but God has made you responsible for another – mine.'

Fallon's face was very pale now. He took a step back, turned and walked towards the hoist without a word. As he drew abreast of a buttress, some slight noise caused him to look to his left and he saw Anna da Costa hiding behind it.

He drew her out gently, but in spite of that fact, she cried out in fear. Fallon said softly. 'It's all right. I promise you.'

Father da Costa hurried forward and pulled her away from him. 'Leave her alone.'

Anna started to weep softly as he held her

73

in his arms. Fallon stood looking at them, a slight frown on his face. 'Perhaps she's heard more than was good for her.'

Father da Costa held Anna away from him a little and looked down at her. 'Is that so?'

She nodded, whispering, 'I was in the church.' She turned reaching out her hands, feeling her way to Fallon. 'What kind of man are you?'

One hand found his face as he stood there as if turned to stone. She drew back hastily as if stung and da Costa put a protective arm about her again.

'Leave us!' she whispered hoarsely to Fallon. 'I'll say nothing of what I heard to anyone, I promise, only go away and don't come back. Please!' There was a passionate entreaty in her voice.

Father da Costa held her close again and Fallon said, 'Does she mean it?'

'She said, didn't she?' Father da Costa told him. 'We take your guilt on our souls, Fallon. Now get out of here.'

Fallon showed no emotion at all. He turned and walked to the hoist. As he opened the gate, da Costa called, 'Two of us now, Fallon. Two lives to be responsible for. Are you up to that?'

Fallon stood there for a long moment, a hand on the open gate. Finally, he said softly, 'It will be all right. I gave you my word. My own life on it, if you like.'

He stepped into the hoist and closed the gate. There was the gentle whirring of the electric motor, a dull echo from below as the cage reached the ground floor.

Anna looked up. 'He's gone?' she whispered.

Father da Costa nodded. 'It's all right now.'

'He was in the church earlier,' she said. 'He told me what was wrong with the organ. Isn't that the strangest thing?'

'The organ?' Da Costa stared down at her in bewilderment and then he sighed, shaking his head and turned her gently round. 'Come on, now, I'll take you home. You'll catch your death.'

They stood at the cage, waiting for the gate to come up after he had pressed the button. Anna said slowly, 'What are we going to do, Uncle Michael?'

'About Martin Fallon?' He put an arm about her shoulder. 'For the moment, nothing. What he told me in the church spilled over from the confessional box because of my anger and impatience so that what you over-heard was still strictly part of that original confession. I'm afraid I can't look at it in any other way.' He sighed. 'I'm sorry, Anna. I know this must be an intolerable burden for you, but I must ask you to give me your promise not to speak of this to anyone.'

'But I already have,' she said. 'To him.'

A strange thing to say and it troubled him deeply as the cage arrived and they moved inside and made the quick descent to the church.

Alone in his study, he did a thing he seldom did so early in the day and poured himself a glass of whisky. He sipped it slowly and stood, one hand on the marble mantelpiece and stared down into the flames of the small coal fire.

'And what do we do now, Michael?' he asked himself softly.

It was an old habit, this carrying on a conversation with his inner self. A relic of three years of solitary confinement in a Chinese prison cell in North Korea. Useful in any situation where he needed to be as objective as possible about some close personal problem.

But then, in a sense, this wasn't his problem, it was Fallon's, he saw that suddenly with startling clarity. His own situation was such that his hands were tied. There was little that he could do or say. The next move would have to be Fallon's.

There was a knock at the door and Anna appeared. 'Superintendent Miller to see you, Uncle Michael.'

Miller moved into the room, hat in hand. 'There you are, Superintendent,' da Costa said. 'Have you met my niece?'

He made a formal introduction. Anna was remarkably controlled. In fact she showed no nervousness at all, which surprised him.

'I'll leave you to it.' She hesitated, the door half-open. 'You'll be going out, then?'

'Not just yet,' Father da Costa told her.

Miller frowned. 'But I don't understand, Father, I thought . . . .'

'A moment, please, Superintendent,' Father da Costa said and glanced at Anna. She went out, closing the door softly and he turned again to Miller. 'You were saying?'

'Our arrangement was that you were to come down to the Department to look at some photos,' Miller said.

'I know, Superintendent, but that won't be possible now.'

'May I ask why not, Father?' Miller demanded.

Father da Costa had given considerable thought to his answer, yet in the end could manage nothing more original than, 'I'm afraid I wouldn't be able to help you, that's all.'

Miller was genuinely puzzled and showed it. 'Let's start again, Father. Perhaps you didn't understand me properly. All I want you to do is to come down to the Department to look at some photos in the hope that you might recognise our friend of this morning.'

'I know all that,' Father da Costa told him.

'And you still refuse to come?'

'There wouldn't be any point.'

'Why not?'

'Because I can't help you.'

For a moment, Miller genuinely thought he was going out of his mind. This couldn't be happening. It just didn't make any kind of sense, and then he was struck by a sudden, dreadful suspicion.

'Has Meehan been getting at you in some way?'

'Meehan?' Father da Costa said, his genuine bewilderment so perfectly obvious that Miller immediately dropped the whole idea.

'I could have you brought in formally, Father, as a material witness.'

'You can take a horse to water but you can't make him drink, Superintendent.'

'I can have a damn good try,' Miller told him grimly. He walked to the door and opened it. 'Don't make me take you in formally, sir. I'd rather not but I will if I have to.'

'Superintendent Miller,' Father da Costa said softly, 'men of a harsher disposition than you have tried to make me speak in circumstances where it was not appropriate. They did not succeed and neither will you, I can assure you. No power on earth can make me speak on this matter if I do not wish to.'

'We'll see about that, sir. I'll give you some time to think this matter over, then I'll be back.' He was about to walk out when a sudden wild thought struck him and he turned, slowly, 'Have you seen him again, sir, since this morning? Have you been threatened? Is your life in any kind of danger?'

'Goodbye, Superintendent,' Father da Costa said.

The front door banged. Father da Costa turned to finish his whisky and Anna moved silently into the room. She put a hand on his arm.

'He'll go to Monsignor O'Halloran.'

'The bishop being at present in Rome, that would seem the obvious thing to do.' he said.

'Hadn't you better get there first?'

'I suppose so.' He emptied his glass and put it on the mantel-piece. 'What about you?'

80

'I want to do some more organ practice. I'll be all right.'

She pushed him out into the hall and reached for his coat from the stand with unerring aim. 'What would I do without you?' he said.

She smiled cheerfully. 'Goodness knows. Hurry back.'

He went out, she closed the door after him. When she turned, the smile had completely disappeared. She went back into his study, sat down by the fire and buried her face in her hands.

Nick Miller had been a policeman for almost a quarter of a century. Twenty-five years of working a three-shift system. Of being disliked by his neighbours, of being able to spend only one weekend in seven at home with his family and the consequent effect upon his relationship with his son and daughter.

He had little formal education but he was a shrewd, clever man with the ability to cut through to the heart of things, and this, coupled with an extensive knowledge of human nature gained from a thousand long, hard Saturday nights on the town, had made him a good policeman.

He had no conscious thought or even desire to help society. His job was in the main to catch thieves, and society consisted of the civilians who sometimes got mixed up in the constant state of guerrilla warfare which existed between the police and the criminal. If anything, he preferred the criminal. At least you knew where you were with him.

But Dandy Jack Meehan was different. One corruption was all corruption, he'd read that somewhere and if it applied to any human being, it applied to Meehan.

Miller loathed him with the kind of obsessive hate that was in the end self-destructive. To be precise, ten years of his life had gone to Dandy Jack without the slightest hint of success. Meehan had to be behind the Krasko killing, that was a fact of life. The rivalry between the two men had been common knowledge for at least two years.

For the first time in God knows how long he'd had a chance and now, the priest . . .

When he got into the rear of the car he was shaking with anger, and on a sudden impulse he leaned across and told his driver to take him to the headquarters of Meehan's funeral business. Then he sat back and tried to light his pipe with trembling fingers.

5

Dandy Jack

Paul's Square was a green lung in the heart
of the city, an acre of grass and flower-beds
and willow trees with a fountain in the centre
surrounded on all four sides by Georgian
terrace houses, most of which were used as
offices by barristers, solicitors or doctors and
beautifully preserved.

There was a general atmosphere of quiet
dignity and Meehan's funeral business fitted
in perfectly. Three houses on the north side
had been converted to provide every possible
facility from a flower shop to a Chapel of
Rest. A mews entrance to one side gave
access to a car park and garage area at the
rear surrounded by high walls so that
business could be handled as quietly and as

unobtrusively as possible, a facility which had other uses on occasion.

When the big Bentley hearse turned into the car park shortly after one o'clock, Meehan was sitting up front with the chauffeur and Billy. He wore his usual double-breasted melton overcoat and Homburg hat and a black tie for he had been officiating personally at a funeral that morning.

The chauffeur came round to open the door and Meehan got out followed by his brother. 'Thanks, Donner,' he said.

A small grey whippet was drinking from a dish at the rear entrance. Billy called, 'Here, Tommy!' It turned, hurled itself across the yard and jumped into his arms.

Billy fondled its ears and it licked his face frantically. 'Now then, you little bastard,' he said with genuine affection.

'I've told you before,' Meehan said. 'He'll ruin your coat. Hairs all over the bloody place.'

As he moved towards the rear entrance, Varley came out of the garage and stood waiting for him, cap in hand. A muscle twitched nervously in his right cheek, his forehead was beaded with sweat. He seemed almost on the point of collapse.

Meehan paused, hands in pockets and looked him over calmly. 'You look awful, Charlie. You been a bad lad or something?'

'Not me, Mr Meehan,' Vatley said. 'It's that sod, Fallon. He . . .'

'Not here, Charlie,' Meehan said softly. 'I always like to hear bad news in private.'

He nodded to Donner who opened the rear door and stood to one side. Meehan went into what was usually referred to as the receiving-room. It was empty except for a coffin on a trolley in the centre.

He put a cigarette in his mouth and bent down to read the brass nameplate on the coffin.

'When's this for?'

Donner moved to his side, a lighter ready in his hand. 'Three-thirty, Mr Meehan.'

He spoke with an Australian accent and had a slightly twisted mouth, the scar still plain where a hair lip had been cured by plastic surgery. It gave him a curiously repellent appearance, modified to a certain extent by the hand-tailored, dark uniform suit he wore.

'Is it a cremation?'

Donner shook his head. 'A burial, Mr Meehan.'

Meehan nodded. 'All right, you and Bonati better handle it. I've an idea I'm going to be busy.'

He turned, one arm on the coffin. Billy leaned against the wall, fondling the whippet. Varley waited in the centre of the room, cap in hand, the expression on his face that of a condemned man waiting for the trap to open beneath his feet at any moment and plunge him into eternity.

'All right, Charlie,' Meehan said. 'Tell me the worst.'

Varley told him, the words falling over themselves in his eagerness to get them out. When he had finished, there was a lengthy silence. Meehan had shown no emotion at all.

'So he's coming here at two o'clock?'

'That's what he said, Mr Meehan.'

'And the van? You took it to the wrecker's yard like I told you?'

'Saw it go into the crusher myself, just like you said.'

Varley waited for his sentence, face damp with sweat. Meehan smiled suddenly and patted him on the cheek. 'You did well, Charlie. Not your fault things went wrong. Leave it to me. I'll handle it.'

Relief seemed to ooze out of Varley like dirty water. He said weakly, 'Thanks, Mr Meehan. I did my best. Honest I did. You know me.'

'You have something to eat,' Meehan said. 'Then get back to the car wash. If I need you, I'll send for you.'

Varley went out. The door closed. Billy giggled as he fondled the whippet's ears. 'I told you he was trouble. We could have handled it ourselves only you wouldn't listen.'

Meehan grabbed him by the long white hair, the boy cried out in pain, dropping the dog. 'Do you want me to get nasty, Billy?' he said softly. 'Is that what you want?'

'I didn't mean any harm, Jack,' the boy whined.

Meehan shoved him away. 'Then be a good

boy. Tell Bonati I want him, then take one of the cars and go and get Fat Albert.'

Billy's tongue flicked nervously between his lips. 'Albert?' he whispered. 'For God's sake, Jack, you know I can't stand being anywhere near that big creep. He frightens me to death.'

'That's good,' Meehan said. 'I'll remember that next time you step out of line. We'll call Albert in to take you in hand.' He laughed harshly. 'Would you like that?'

Billy's eyes were wide with fear. 'No, please, Jack,' he whispered. 'Not Albert.'

'Be a good lad, then.' Meehan patted his face and opened the door. 'On your way.'

Billy went out and Meehan turned to Donner with a sigh. 'I don't know what I'm going to do with him, Frank. I don't really.'

'He's young, Mr Meehan.'

'All he can think about is birds,' Meehan said. 'Dirty little tarts in mini skirts showing all they've got.' He shivered in genuine disgust. 'I even found him having it off with the cleaning woman one afternoon. Fifty-five if she was a day – and on my bed.'

Donner kept a diplomatic silence and

Meehan opened an inner door and led the way through into the Chapel of Rest. The stmosphere was cool and fresh thanks to air-conditioning, and scented with flowers. Taped organ music provided a suitably devotional background.

There were half-a-dozen cubicles on either side. Meehan took off his hat and stepped into the first one. There were flowers everywhere and an oak coffin stood on a draped trolley.

'Who's this?'

'That young girl. The student who went through the windscreen of the sports car,' Donner told him.

'Oh yes,' Meehan said. 'I did her myself.'

He lifted the face cloth. The girl was perhaps eighteen or nineteen, eyes closed, lips slightly parted, the face so skilfully made up that she might only have been sleeping.

'You did a good job there, Mr Meehan,' Donner said.

Meehan nodded complacently. 'I've got to agree with you there, Frank. You know something. There was no flesh left on her left cheek

90

when she came to me. That girl's face was mincemeat, I'm telling you.'

'You're an artist, Mr Meehan,' Donner said, genuine admiration in his voice. 'A real artist. It's the only word for it.'

'It's nice of you to say so, Frank. I really appreciate that.' Meehan switched off the light and led the way out. 'I always try to do my best, of course, but a case like that – a young girl. Well, you got to think of the parents.'

'Too true, Mr Meehan.'

They moved out of the chapel area into the front hall, the original Georgian features still beautifully preserved, blue and white Wedgwood plaques on the walls. There was a glass door leading to the reception office on the right. As they approached, they could hear voices and someone appeared to be crying.

The door opened and a very old woman appeared, sobbing heavily. She wore a head-scarf and a shabby woollen overcoat bursting at the seams. She had a carrier bag over one arm and clutched a worn leather purse in her left hand. Her face was swollen with weeping.

Henry Ainsley, the reception clerk, moved out after her. He was a tall, thin man with hollow cheeks and sly, furtive eyes. He wore a neat, clerical-grey suit and sober tie and his hands were soft.

'I'm sorry, madam,' he was saying sharply, 'but that's the way it is. Anyway, you can leave everything in our hands from now on.'

'That's the way what is?' Meehan said, advancing on them. He put his hands on the old lady's shoulders. 'We can't have this, love. What's up?'

'It's all right, Mr Meehan. The old lady was just a bit upset. She's just lost her husband,' Ainsley said.

Meehan ignored him and drew the old lady into the office. He put her in a chair by the desk. 'Now then, love, you tell me all about it.'

He took her hand and she held on tight. 'Ninety, he was. I thought he'd last for ever and then I found him at the bottom of the stairs when I got back from chapel, Sunday night.' Tears streamed down her face.

'He was that strong, even at that age. I couldn't believe it.'

'I know, love, and now you've come here to bury him?'

She nodded. 'I don't have much, but I didn't want him to have a state funeral. I wanted it done right. I thought I could manage nicely what the insurance money and then this gentleman here, he told me I'd need seventy pound.'

'Now look, Mr Meehan, it was like this,' Ainsley cut in.

Meehan turned and glanced at him bleakly. Ainsley faltered into silence. Meehan said, 'You paid cash, love?'

'Oh yes,' she said. 'I called at the insurance office on the way and they paid me out on the policy. Fifty pounds, I thought it would be enough.'

'And the other twenty?'

'I had twenty-five pounds in the Post Office.'

'I see.' Meehan straightened. 'Show me the file,' he said.

Ainsley stumbled to the desk and picked

up a small sheaf of papers which shook a little as he held them out. Meehan leafed through them. He smiled delightedly and put a hand on the old woman's shoulders.

'I've got good news for you, love. There's been a mistake.'

'A mistake?' she said.

He took out his wallet and extracted twenty-five pounds. 'Mr Ainsley was forgetting about the special rate we've been offering to old age pensioners this autumn.'

She looked at the money, a dazed expression on her face. 'Special rate. Here, it won't be a state funeral will it? I wouldn't want that.'

Meehan helped her to her feet. 'Not on your life. Private. The best. I guarantee it. Now let's go and see about your flowers.'

'Flowers?' she said. 'Oh, that would be nice. He loved flowers, did my Bill.'

'All included, love.' Meehan glanced over his shoulder at Donner. 'Keep him here. I'll be back.'

A door had been cut through the opposite wall giving access to the flower shop next door. When Meehan ushered the old lady in, they were immediately approached by a tall, willowy young man with shoulder-length dark hair and a beautiful mouth.

'Yes, Mr Meehan. Can I be of service?' He spoke with a slight lisp.

Meehan patted his cheek. 'You certainly can, Rupert. Help this good lady choose a bunch of flowers. Best in the shop and a wreath. On the firm, of course.'

Rupert accepted the situation without the slightest question. 'Certainly, Mr Meehan.'

'And Rupert, see one of the lads runs her home afterwards.' He turned to the old lady. 'All right, love?'

She reached up and kissed his cheek. 'You're a good man. A wonderful man. God bless you.'

'He does, my love,' Dandy Jack Meehan told her. 'Every day of my life.' And he walked out.

'Death is something you've got to have some respect for,' Meehan said. 'I mean, this old lady. According to the form she's filled in,

95

she's eighty-three. I mean, that's a wonderful thing.'

He was sitting in the swing chair in front of the desk. Henry Ainsley stood in front of him, Donner was by the door.

Ainsley stirred uneasily and forced a smile, 'Yes, I see what you mean, Mr Meehan.'

'Do you, Henry? I wonder.'

There was a knock at the door and a small, dapper man in belted continental raincoat entered. He looked like a Southern Italian, but spoke with a South Yorkshire accent.

'You wanted me, Mr Meehan?'

'That's it, Bonati. Come in.' Meehan returned to Ainsley. 'Yes, I really wonder about you, Henry. Now the way I see it, this was an insurance job. She's strictly working class. The policy pays fifty and you price the job at seventy and the old dear coughs up because she can't stand the thought of her Bill having a state funeral.' He shook his head. 'You gave her a receipt for fifty, which she's too tired and old to notice, and you enter fifty in the cash book.'

Ainsley was shaking like a leaf. 'Please,

Mr Meehan, please listen. I've had certain difficulties lately.'

Meehan stood up. 'Has he been brought in, her husband?'

Ainsley nodded. 'This morning. He's in number three. He hasn't been prepared yet.'

'Bring him along,' Meehan told Donner and walked out.

He went into cubicle number three in the Chapel of Rest and switched on the light and the others followed him in. The old man was laying in an open coffin with a sheet over him and Meehan pulled it away. He was quite naked and had obviously been a remarkably powerful man in his day with the shoulders and chest of a heavyweight wrestler.

Meehan looked at him in awe. 'He was a bull this one and no mistake. Look at the dick on him.' He turned to Ainsley. 'Think of the women he pleasured. Think of that old lady. By God, I can see why she loved him. He was a man, this old lad.'

His knee came up savagely. Henry Ainsley grabbed for his privates too late and he pitched forward with a choked cry.

'Take him up to the coffin room,' Meehan told Donner. 'I'll join you in five minutes.'

When Henry Ainsley regained his senses, he was lying flat on his back, arms outstretched, Donner standing on one hand, Bonati on the other.

The door opened and Meehan entered. He stood looking down at him for a moment, then nodded. 'All right, pick him up.'

The room was used to store coffins which weren't actually made on the premises, but there were a couple of workbenches and a selection of carpenter's tools on a rack on the wall.

'Please, Mr Meehan,' Ainsley begged him.

Meehan nodded to Donner and Bonati dragged Ainsley back across one of the workbenches, arms outstretched, palms uppermost.

Meehan stood over him. 'I'm going to teach you a lesson, Henry. Not because you tried to fiddle me out of twenty quid. That's one thing that's definitely not allowed, but it's more than that. You see, I'm thinking of that old girl. She's never had a thing in her life. All she ever got was screwed into the ground.'

His eyes were smoking now and there was a slightly dreamy quality to his voice. 'She reminded me of my old mum, I don't know why. But I know one thing. She's earned some respect just like her old fella's earned something better than a state funeral.'

'You've got it wrong, Mr Meehan,' Ainsley gabbled.

'No, Henry, you're the one who got it wrong.'

Meehan selected two bradawls from the rack on the wall. He tested the point of one on his thumb then drove it through the centre of Ainsley's right palm pinning his hand to the bench. When he repeated the process with the other hand Ainsley fainted.

Meehan turned to Donner. 'Five minutes, then release him and tell him if he isn't in the office on time in the morning, I'll have his balls.'

'All right, Mr Meehan,' Donner said. 'What about Fallon?'

'I'll be in the preparation room. I've got some embalming to do. When Fallon comes, keep him in the office till I've had a chance to get up to the flat, then bring him up. And I want Albert up there as soon as he comes in.'

'Kid glove treatment, Mr Meehan?'

'What else, Frank? What else?'

Meehan smiled, patted the unconscious Ainsley on the cheek and walked out.

The preparation room was on the other side of the Chapel of Rest and when Meehan went in he closed the door. He liked to be alone on such occasions. It aided concentration and made the whole thing somehow much more personal.

A body waited for him on the table in the centre of the room covered with a sheet. Beside it on a trolley the tools of his trade were laid out neatly on a white cloth. Scalpels, scissors, forceps, surgical needles of various sizes, artery tubes, a large rubber bulb syringe and a glass jar containing a couple of gallons of embalming fluid. On a shelf underneath was an assortment of cosmetics, make-up creams and face powders, all made to order.

He pulled away the sheet and folded it neatly. The body was that of a woman of forty – handsome, dark-haired. He remembered the case. A history of heart trouble. She'd died in mid-sentence while discussing plans for Christmas with her husband.

There was still that look of faint surprise on her face that many people show in death; jaw dropped, mouth gaping as if in amazement that this should be happening to her of all people.

Meehan took a long curved needle and skilfully passed a thread from behind the lower lip, up through the nasal septum and down again, so that when he tightened the thread and tied it off, the jaw was raised.

The eyeballs had fallen into their sockets. He compensated for that by inserting a circle of cotton wool under each eyelid before closing it and cotton wool between the lips and gums and in the cheeks to give a fuller, more natural appearance.

All this he did with total absorption,

whistling softly between his teeth, a frown of concentration on his face. His anger at Ainsley had disappeared totally. Even Fallon had ceased to exist. He smeared a little cream on the cold lips with one finger, stood back and nodded in satisfaction. He was now ready to start the embalming process.

The body weighed nine and a half stones which meant that he needed about eleven pints of fluid of the mixture he habitually used. Formaldehyde, glycerine, borax with a little phenol added and some sodium citrate as an anti-coagulant.

It was a simple enough case with little likelihood of complications so he decided to start with the axillary artery as usual. He extended the left arm at right angles to the body, the elbow supported on a wooden block, reached for a scalpel and made his first incision halfway between the mid-point of the collar-bone and the bend of the elbow.

It was perhaps an hour later as he tied off the last stitch that he became aware of some sort of disturbance outside. Voices were raised in anger and then the door flew open. Meehan glanced over his shoulder. Miller was standing there. Billy tried to squeeze past him.

'I tried to stop him, Jack.'

'Make some tea,' Meehan told him. 'I'm thirsty. And close that door. You'll ruin the temperature in here. How many times have I told you?'

Billy retired, the door closing softly behind him and Meehan turned back to the body. He reached for a jar of foundation cream and started to rub some into the face of the dead woman with infinite gentleness, ignoring Miller completely.

Miller lit a cigarette, the match rasping in the silence and Meehan said without turning round, 'Not in here. In here we show a little respect.'

'Is that a fact?' Miller replied, but he still dropped the cigarette on the floor and stepped on it.

He approached the table. Meehan was now applying a medium red cream rouge to the woman's cheekbones, his fingers bringing her back to life by the minute.

Miller watched for a moment in fascinated horror. 'You really like your work, don't you, Jack?'

'What do you want?' Meehan asked calmly.

'You.'

'Nothing new in that, is there?' Meehan replied. 'I mean, anybody falls over and breaks a leg in this town you come to me.'

'All right,' Miller said. 'So we'll go through the motions. Jan Krasko went up to the cemetery this morning to put flowers on his mother's grave. He's been doing that for just over a year now – every Thursday without fail.'

'So the bastard has a heart after all. Why tell me?'

'At approximately ten past eleven somebody put a bullet through his skull. A real pro job. Nice and public, so everyone would get the message.'

'And what message would that be?'

'Toe the Meehan line or else.'

104

Meehan dusted the face with powder calmly. 'I had a funeral this morning,' he said. 'Old Marcus the draper. At ten past eleven I was sitting in St Saviour's listening to the vicar say his piece. Ask Billy – he was with me. Along with around a couple of hundred other people including the mayor. He had a lot of friends had old Mr Marcus, but then he was a gentleman. Not many of his kind left these days.'

He brightened the eyebrows and lashes with Vaseline and coloured the lips. The effect was truly remarkable. The woman seemed only to sleep.

Miller said, 'I don't care where you were. It was your killing.'

Meehan turned to face him, wiping his hands on a towel. 'Prove it,' he said flatly.

All the frustration of the long years, all the anger, welled up in Miller threatening to choke him so that he pulled at his tie, wrenching open his collar.

'I'll get you for this, Meehan,' he said. 'I'll lay it on you if it's the last thing I do. This time you've gone too far.'

Meehan's eyes became somehow luminous, his entire personality assumed a new dimension, power seemed to emanate from him like electricity.

'You – touch me?' He laughed coldly, turned and gestured to the woman. 'Look at her, Miller. She was dead. I've given her life again. And you think you can touch me?'

Miller took at involuntary step back and Meehan cried, 'Go on, get the hell out of it!'

And Miller went as if all the devils in hell had been snapping at his heels.

It was suddenly very quiet in the preparation room. Meehan stood there, chest heaving, and then reached for the tin of vanishing cream and turned to the woman.

'I gave you life again,' he whispered. 'Life.'

He started to rub the cream firmly into the body.

6

Face to Face

It was still raining when Fallon crossed Paul's Square and went up the steps to the main entrance. When he tried the office it was empty and then Rupert appeared, having noticed him arrive through the glass door of the flower shop.

'Can I help you, sir?'

'Fallon's the name. Meehan's expecting me.'

'Oh yes, sir.' Rupert was exquisitely polite. 'If you'd like to wait in the office I'll just see where he is.'

He went out and Fallon lit a cigarette and waited. It was a good ten minutes before Rupert reappeared.

'I'll take you up now, sir,' he said, and with a flashing smile led the way out into the hall.

'And where would up be?' Fallon asked him.

'Mr Meehan's had the attics of the three houses knocked together into a penthouse suite for his personal use. Beautiful.'

They reached a small lift and as Rupert opened the door Fallon said, 'Is this the only way?'

'There's the back stairs.'

'Then the back stairs it is.'

Rupert's ready smile slipped a little. 'Now don't start to play games, ducky. It'll only get Mr Meehan annoyed, which means I'll end up having one hell of a night and to be perfectly frank, I'm not in the mood.'

'I'd have thought you'd have enjoyed every golden moment,' Fallon said and kicked him very hard on the right shin.

Rupert cried out and went down on one knee and Fallon took the Ceska out of his right-hand pocket. He had removed the silencer, but it was still a deadly-looking item in every way. Rupert went white, but he was game to the last.

'He'll crucify you for this. Nobody mixes

it with Jack Meehan and passes the post first.'

Fallon put the Ceska back in his pocket. 'The stairs,' he said softly.

'All right,' Rupert leaned down to rub his shin. 'It's your funeral, ducky.'

The stairway started beside the entrance to the Chapel of Rest and they climbed three flights, Rupert leading the way. There was a green baize door at the top and he paused a few steps below. 'That leads directly into the kitchen.'

Fallon nodded. 'You'd better go back to minding the shop then, hadn't you?'

Rupert needed no second bidding and went back down the stairs quickly. Fallon tried the door which opened to his touch. As Rupert had said, a kitchen was on the other side. The far door stood ajar and he could hear voices.

He crossed to it on tiptoe and looked into a superbly furnished lounge with broad dormer windows at either end. Meehan was sitting in a leather club chair, a book in one hand, a glass of whisky in the other. Billy, holding the whippet, stood in front of an Adam fireplace in which a log fire was burning brightly. Donner and Bonati waited on either side of the lift.

'What's keeping him, for Christ's sake?' Billy demanded.

The whippet jumped from his arms and darted across to the kitchen door. It stood there, barking, and Fallon moved into the lounge and crouched down to fondle its ears, his right hand still in his coat pocket.

Meehan dropped the book on the table and slapped a hand against his thigh. 'Didn't I tell you he was a hard-nosed bastard?' he said to Billy.

The telephone rang. He picked it up, listened for a moment and smiled. 'It's all right, sweetheart, you get back to work. I can handle it.' He replaced the receiver. 'That was Rupert. He worries about me.'

'That's nice,' Fallon said.

He leaned against the wall beside the kitchen door, hands in pockets. Donner and Bonati moved in quietly and stood behind the big leather couch facing him. Meehan

110

sipped a little of his whisky and held up the book. It was *The City of God* by St Augustine.

'Read this one, have you, Fallon?'

'A long time ago.' Fallon reached for a cigarette with his left hand.

'It's good stuff,' Meehan said. 'He knew what he was talking about. God and the Devil, good and evil. They all exist. And sex.' He emptied his glass and belched. 'He really puts the record straight there. I mean, women just pump a man dry, like I keep trying to tell my little brother here only he won't listen. Anything in a skirt, he goes for. You ever seen a dog after a bitch in heat with it hanging half out? Well, that's our Billy twenty-four hours a day.'

He poured himself another whisky and Fallon waited. They all waited. Meehan stared into space. 'No, these dirty little tarts are no good to anybody and the boys are no better. I mean, what's happened to all the nice clean-cut lads of sixteen or seventeen you used to see around? These days, most of them look like birds from the rear.'

Fallon said nothing. There was a further

111

silence and Meehan reached for the whisky bottle again. 'Albert!' he called. 'Why don't you join us?'

The bedroom door opened, there was a pause and a man entered the room who was so large that he had to duck his head to come through the door. He was a walking anachronism. Neanderthal man in a baggy grey suit and he must have weighed at least twenty stone. His head was completely bald and his arms were so long that his hands almost reached his knees.

He shambled into the room, his little pig eyes fixed on Fallon. Billy moved out of the way nervously and Albert sank into a chair on the other side of Meehan, next to the fire.

Meehan said, 'All right, Fallon. You cocked it up.'

'You wanted Krasko dead. He's on a slab in the mortuary right now,' Fallon said.

'And the priest who saw you in action? This Father da Costa?'

'No problem.'

'He can identify you, can't he? Varley says

he was close enough to count the wrinkles on your face.'

'True enough,' Fallon said. 'But it doesn't matter. I've shut his mouth.'

'You mean you've knocked him off?' Billy demanded.

'No need.' Fallon turned to Meehan. 'Are you a Catholic?'

Meehan nodded, frowning. 'What's that got to do with it?'

'When did you last go to confession?'

'How in the hell do I know? It's so long ago I forget.'

'I went today,' Fallon said. 'That's where I've been. I waited my turn at da Costa's one o'clock confession. When I went in, I told him I'd shot Krasko.'

Billy Meehan said quickly, 'But that's crazy. He'd seen you do it himself, hadn't he?'

'But he didn't know it was me in that confessional box – not until he looked through the grille and recognised me and that was after I'd confessed.'

'So what, for Christ's sake?' Billy demanded.

But his brother was already waving him down, his face serious. 'I get it,' he said. 'Of course. Anything said to a priest at confession's got to be kept a secret. I mean, they guarantee that, don't they?'

'Exactly,' Fallon said.

'It's the biggest load of cobblers I've ever heard,' Billy said. 'He's alive, isn't he? And he knows. What guarantee do you have that he won't suddenly decide to shoot his mouth off?'

'Let's just say it isn't likely,' Fallon said. 'And even if he did, it wouldn't matter. I'm being shipped out from Hull Sunday night – or have you forgotten?'

Meehan said, 'I don't know. Maybe Billy has a point.'

'Billy couldn't find his way to the men's room unless you took him by the hand,' Fallon told him flatly.

There was a dead silence. Meehan gazed at him impassively and Albert picked a steel and brass poker out of the fireplace and bent it into a horseshoe shape between his great hands, his eyes never leaving Fallon's face.

Meehan chuckled unexpectedly. 'That's good – that's very good. I like that.'

He got up, walked to a desk in the corner, unlocked it and took out a large envelope. He returned to his chair and dropped the envelope on the coffee table.

'There's fifteen hundred quid in there,' he said. 'You get another two grand on board ship Sunday night plus a passport. That clears the account.'

'That's very civil of you,' Fallon said.

'Only one thing,' Meehan told him. 'The priest goes.'

Fallon shook his head. 'Not a chance.'

'What's wrong with you, then?' Meehan jeered. 'Worried, are you? Afraid the Almighty might strike you down? They told me you were big stuff over there, Fallon, running round Belfast, shooting soldiers and blowing up kids. But a priest is different, is that it?'

Fallon said, in what was little more than a whisper, 'Nothing happens to the priest. That's the way I want it. That's the way it's going to be.'

'The way *you* want it?' Meehan said and

the anger was beginning to break through now.

Albert tossed the poker into the fireplace and stood up. He spoke in a rough, hoarse voice. 'Which arm shall I break first, Mr Meehan? His left or his right?'

Fallon pulled out the Ceska and fired instantly. The bullet splintered Albert's right kneecap and he went back over the chair. He lay there cursing, clutching his knee with both hands, blood pumping between his fingers.

For a moment, nobody moved and then Meehan laughed out loud. 'Didn't I tell you he was beautiful?' he said to Billy.

Fallon picked up the envelope and stowed it away in his raincoat. He backed into the kitchen without a word, kicked the door shut as Meehan called out to him and started down the stairs.

In the lounge, Meehan grabbed his coat and made for the lift. 'Come on, Billy!'

As he got the door open, Donner called, 'What about Albert?'

'Call that Pakistani doctor. The one who was struck off. He'll fix him up.'

116

As the lift dropped to the ground floor Billy said, 'Look, what are we up to?'

'Just follow me and do as you're bleeding well told,' Meehan said.

He ran along the corridor, through the hall and out of the front door. Fallon had reached the other side of the road and was taking one of the paths that led across the green centre of the square.

Meehan called to him and ran across the road, ignoring the traffic. The Irishman glanced over his shoulder but kept on walking and had reached the fountain before Meehan and Billy caught up with him.

He turned to face them, his right hand in his pocket and Meehan put up a hand defensively. 'I just want to talk.'

He dropped on to a bench seat, slightly breathless, and took out a handkerchief to wipe his face. Billy arrived a moment later just as the rain increased suddenly from a steady drizzle into a solid downpour.

He said, 'This is crazy. My bloody suit's going to be ruined.'

His brother ignored him and grinned up

at Fallon disarmingly. 'You're hell on wheels, aren't you, Fallon? There isn't a tearaway in town who wouldn't run from Fat Albert, but you.' He laughed uproariously. 'You put him on sticks for six months.'

'He shouldn't have joined,' Fallon said.

'Too bloody true, but to hell with Albert. You were right, Fallon, about the priest, I mean.' Fallon showed no emotion at all, simply stood there watching him and Meehan laughed. 'Scout's honour. I won't lay a glove on him.'

'I see,' Fallon said. 'A change of heart?'

'Exactly, but it still leaves us with a problem. What to do with you till that boat leaves Sunday. I think maybe you should go back to the farm.'

'No chance,' Fallon said.

'Somehow I thought you might say that.' Meehan smiled good-humouredly. 'Still, we've got to find you something.' He turned to Billy. 'What about Jenny? Jenny Fox. Couldn't she put him up?'

'I suppose so,' Billy said sullenly.

'A nice kid,' Meehan told Fallon. 'She's

worked for me in the past. I helped her out when she was having a kid. She owes me a favour.'

'She's a whore,' Billy said.

'So what?' Meehan shrugged. 'A nice, safe house and not too far away. Billy can run you up there.'

He smiled genially – even the eyes smiled – but Fallon wasn't taken in for a moment. On the other hand, the sober truth was that he did need somewhere to stay.

'All right,' he said.

Meehan put an arm around his shoulders. 'You couldn't do better. She cooks like a dream, that girl, and when it comes to dropping her pants she's a little firecracker, I can tell you.'

They went back across the square and followed the mews round to the car park at the rear. The whippet was crouched at the entrance, shivering in the rain. When Billy appeared, it ran to heel and followed him into the garage. When he drove out in a scarlet Scimitar, it was sitting in the rear.

Fallon slipped into the passenger seat and

Meehan closed the door. 'I'd stick pretty close to home if I were you. No sense in running any needless risks at this stage, is there?'

Fallon didn't say a word and Billy drove away. The door to the reception room opened and Donner came out. 'I've rung for that quack, Mr Meehan. What happened to Fallon?'

'Billy's taking him up to Jenny Fox's place,' Meehan said. 'I want you to go over to the car wash and get hold of Varley. I want him outside Jenny's place within half an hour. If Fallon leaves, he follows and phones in whenever he can.'

'I don't follow, Mr Meehan.' Donner was obviously mystified.

'Just till we sort things out, Frank,' Meehan told him. 'Then we drop both of them. Him *and* the priest.'

Donner grinned as a great light dawned. 'That's more like it.'

'I thought you'd approve,' Meehan smiled, opened the door and went inside.

* * *

Jenny Fox was a small, rather hippy girl of nineteen with good breasts, high cheek-bones and almond-shaped eyes. Her straight black hair hung shoulder-length in a dark curtain and the only flaw in the general picture was the fact that she had too much make-up on.

When she came downstairs she was wearing a simple, white blouse, black pleated mini skirt and high-heeled shoes and she walked with a sort of general and total move-ment of the whole body that most men found more than a little disturbing.

Billy Meehan waited for her at the bottom of the stairs and when she was close enough, he slipped a hand up her skirt. She stiffened slightly and he shook his head, a sly, nasty smile on his face.

'Tights again, Jenny. I told you I wanted you to wear stockings.'

'I'm sorry, Billy.' There was fear in her eyes. 'I didn't know you'd be coming today.'

'You'd better watch it, hadn't you, or you'll be getting one of my specials.' She shivered slightly and he withdrew his hand. 'What about Fallon? Did he say anything?'

'Asked me if I had a razor he could borrow. Who is he?'

'None of your business. He shouldn't go out, but if he does, give Jack a ring straight away. And try to find out where he's going.'

'All right, Billy.' She opened the front door for him.

He moved in close behind her, his arms about her waist. She could feel his hardness pressed against her buttocks and the hatred, the loathing rose like bile in her throat, threatening to choke her. He said softly, 'Another thing. Get him into bed. I want to see what makes him tick.'

'And what if he won't play? she said.

'Stocking tops and suspenders. That's what blokes of his age go for. You'll manage.' He slapped her bottom and went out. She closed the door, leaning against it for a moment, struggling for breath. Strange how he always left her with that feeling of suffocation.

She went upstairs, moved along the

corridor and knocked softly on Fallon's door. When she went in, he was standing in front of the washbasin in the corner by the window, drying his hands.

'I'll see if I can find you that razor now,' she said.

He hung the towel neatly over the rail and shook his head. 'It'll do later. I'm going out for a while.'

She was gripped by a sudden feeling of panic. 'Is that wise?' she said. 'I mean, where are you going?'

Fallon smiled as he pulled on his trenchcoat. He ran a finger down her nose in a strangely intimate gesture that brought a lump to her throat.

'Girl dear, do what you have to, which I presume means ringing Jack Meehan to say I'm taking a walk, but I'm damned if I'll say where to.'

'Will you be in for supper?'

'I wouldn't miss it for all the tea in China.' He smiled and was gone.

It was an old-fashioned phrase. One her grandmother had used frequently. She hadn't heard it in years. Strange how it made her want to cry.

When Miller went into the Forensic Department at police headquarters, he found Fitzgerald in the side laboratory with Johnson, the ballistics specialist. Fitzgerald looked excited and Johnson seemed reasonably complacent.

Miller said, 'I hear you've got something for me.'

Johnson was a slow, cautious Scot. 'That just could be, Superintendent.' He picked up a reasonably misshapen piece of lead with a pair of tweezers. 'This is what did all the damage. They found it in the gravel about three yards from the body.'

'Half an hour after you left, sir,' Fitzgerald put in.

'Any hope of making a weapon identification?' Miller demanded.

'Oh, I've pretty well decided that now.' There was a copy of *Small Arms of the World* beside Johnson. He flipped through it quickly, found the page he was searching for and pushed it across to Miller. 'There you are.'

There was a photo of the Ceska in the top right-hand corner. 'I've never even heard of the damn thing,' Miller said. 'How can you be sure?'

'Well, I've some more tests to run, but it's pretty definite. You see there are four factors which are constant in the same make of weapon. Groove and land marks on the bullet, their number and width, their direction, which means are they twisting to the right or left, and the rate of that twist. Once I have those facts, I simply turn to a little item entitled the *Atlas of Arms*, and thanks to the two German gentlemen who so painstakingly put the whole thing together, it's possible to trace the weapon which fits without too much difficulty.'

Miller turned to Fitzgerald. 'Get this information to CRO at Scotland Yard straight away. This Ceska's an out-of-the-way gun. If they feed that into the computer, it might throw out a name. Somebody who's used one before. You never know. I'll see you back in my office.'

Fitzgerald went out quickly and Miller turned to Johnson. 'Anything else, let me know at once.' He went back to his office where he found a file on his desk containing a résumé of Father da Costa's career. Considering the limited amount of time Fitzgerald had had, it was really very comprehensive.

He came in as Miller finished reading the file and closed it. 'I told you he was quite a man, sir.'

'You don't know the half of it,' Miller said and proceeded to tell him what had happened at the presbytery.

Fitzgerald was dumbfounded. 'But it doesn't make any kind of sense.'

'You don't think he's been got at?'

'By Meehan?' Fitzgerald laughed out loud. 'Father da Costa isn't the kind of man who can be got at by anybody. He's the sort who's always spoken up honestly. Said exactly how he felt, even when the person who was hurt most was himself. Look, at his record. He's a brilliant scholar. Two doctorates. One in languages, the other in philosophy, and where's it got him? A dying parish in the heart of a rather unpleasant industrial city. A church that's literally falling down.'

'All right, I'm convinced,' Miller said. 'So he speaks up loud and clear when everyone else has the good sense to keep their mouths shut.' He opened the file again. 'And he's certainly no physical coward. During the war he dropped into Yugoslavia by parachute three times and twice into Albania. DSO in 1944. Wounded twice.' He shrugged impatiently. 'There's got to be an explanation. There must be. It doesn't make any kind of sense that he should refuse to come in like this.'

'But did he actually refuse?'

Miller frowned, trying to remember exactly what the priest had said. 'No, come to think of it, he didn't. He said there was no point to coming in, as he wouldn't be able to help.'

'That's a strange way of putting it,' Fitzgerald said.

'You're telling me. There was an even choicer item. When I told him I could always get a warrant, he said that no power on earth

127

could make him speak on this matter if he
didn't want to.'

Fitzgerald had turned quite pale. He stood
up and leaned across the desk. 'He said that?
You're sure?'

'He certainly did.' Miller frowned. 'Does
it mean something?'

Fitzgerald turned away and moved across
the room to the window. 'I can only think
of one circumstance in which a priest would
speak in such a way.'

'And what would that be?'

'If the information he had at his disposal
had been obtained as part of confession.'

Miller stared at him. 'But that isn't possible.
I mean, he actually saw this character up there
at the cemetery. It wouldn't apply.'

'It could,' Fitzgerald said, 'if the man simply
went into the box and confessed. Da Costa
wouldn't see his face, remember – not then.'

'And you're trying to tell me that once the
bloke has spilled his guts, da Costa would
be hooked?'

'Certainly he would.'

'But that's crazy.'

'Not to a Catholic it isn't. That's the whole point of confession. That what passes between the priest and individual involved, no matter how vile, must be utterly confidential.' He shrugged. 'Just as effective as a bullet, sir.' Fitzgerald hesitated. 'When we were at the cemetery, didn't he tell you he was in a hurry to leave because he had to hear confession at one o'clock?'

Miller was out of his chair and already reaching for his raincoat. 'You can come with me,' he said. 'He might listen to you.'

'What about the autopsy?' Fitzgerald reminded him. 'I thought you wanted to attend personally.'

Miller glanced at his watch. 'There's an hour yet. Plenty of time.'

The lifts were all busy and he went down the stairs two at a time, heart pounding with excitement. Fitzgerald had to be right – it was the only explanation that fitted. But how to handle the situation? That was something else again.

* * *

When Fallon turned down the narrow street beside Holy Name, Varley was no more than thirty yards in the rear. Fallon had been aware of his presence within two minutes of leaving Jenny's place – not that it mattered. He entered the church and Varley made for the phone-box on the corner of the street and was speaking to Meehan within a few moments.

'Mr Meehan? It's me. He's gone into a church in Rockingham Street. The Church of the Holy Name.'

'I'll be there in five minutes,' Meehan said and slammed down the receiver.

He arrived in the scarlet Scimitar with Billy at the wheel to find Varley standing on the street corner, miserable in the rain. He came to meet them as they got out.

'He's still in there, Mr Meehan. I haven't been in myself.'

'Good lad,' Meehan said and glanced up at the church. 'Bloody place looks as if it might fall down at any moment.'

'They serve good soup,' Varley said. 'To dossers. They use the crypt as a day refuge. I've been in. The priest, he's Father da Costa, and his niece, run it between them. She's a blind girl. A real smasher. Plays the organ here.'

Meehan nodded. 'All right, you wait in a doorway. When he comes out, follow him again. Come on, Billy.'

He moved into the porch and opened the door gently. They passed inside and he closed it again quickly.

The girl was playing the organ, he could see the back of her head beyond the green baize curtain. The priest knelt at the altar rail in prayer. Fallon sat at one end of a pew halfway along the aisle.

There was a small chapel to St Martin de Porres on the right. Not a single candle flickered in front of his image, leaving the chapel in semi-darkness. Meehan pulled Billy after him into the concealing shadows and sat down in the corner.

'What in the hell are we supposed to be doing?' Billy whispered.

131

'Just shut up and listen.'

At that moment, Father da Costa stood up and crossed himself. As he turned he saw Fallon.

'There's nothing for you here, you know that,' he said sternly.

Anna stopped playing. She swung her legs over the seat as Fallon advanced along the aisle and Billy whistled softly. 'Christ, did you see those legs?'

'Shut up!' Jack hissed.

'I told you I'd see to things and I have done,' Fallon said as he reached the altar rail. 'I just wanted you to know that.'

'What am I supposed to do, thank you?' Father da Costa said.

The street door banged open, candles flickered in the wind as it closed again and to Jack Meehan's utter astonishment, Miller and Fitzgerald walked up the aisle towards the altar.

'Ah, there you are, Father,' Miller called. 'I'd like a word with you.'

'My God,' Billy Meehan whispered in panic. 'We've got to get out of here.'

'Like hell we do,' Meehan said and his hand gripped Billy's right knee like a vice. 'Just sit still and listen. This could be very interesting.'

7

Prelude and Fugue

Fallon recognised Miller for what he was instantly and waited, shoulders hunched, hands in the pockets of his trenchcoat, feet apart, ready to make whatever move was necessary. There was an elemental force to the man that was almost tangible. Father da Costa could feel it in the very air and the thought of what might happen here filled him with horror.

He moved forward quickly to place himself between Fallon and the two policemen as they approached. Anna paused uncertainly a yard or two on the other side of the altar rail.

Miller stopped, hat in hand, Fitzgerald a pace or two behind him. There was a slight awkward silence and da Costa said, 'I think you've met my niece, Superintendent. He has Inspector Fitzgerald with him, my dear.'

'Miss da Costa,' Miller said formally and turned to Fallon.

Father da Costa said, 'And this is Mr Fallon.'

'Superintendent,' Fallon said easily.

He waited, a slight, fixed smile on his mouth and Miller, looking into that white, intense face, those dark eyes, was aware of a strange, irrational coldness as if somewhere, someone had walked over his grave, which didn't make any kind of sense – and then a sudden, wild thought struck him and he took an involuntary step backwards. There was a silence. Everyone waited. Rain drummed against a window.

It was Anna who broke the spell by taking a blind step towards the altar rail and stumbling. Fallon jumped to catch her.

'Are you all right, Miss da Costa?' he said easily.

'Thank you, Mr Fallon. How stupid of me.' Her slight laugh sounded very convincing as she looked in Miller's general direction. 'I've been having trouble with the organ. I'm

135

afraid that, like the church, it's past its best. Mr Fallon has kindly agreed to give us the benefit of his expert advice.'

'Is that so?' Miller said.

She turned to Father da Costa. 'Do you mind if we start, Uncle? I know Mr Fallon's time is limited.'

'We'll go into the sacristy, if that's all right with you, Superintendent,' Father da Costa said. 'Or up to the house if you prefer.'

'Actually, I'd rather like to hang on here for a few minutes,' Miller told him. 'I'm a pianist myself, but I've always been rather partial to a bit of organ music. If Mr Fallon has no objection.'

Fallon gave him an easy smile. 'Sure and there's nothing like an audience, Superintendent, for bringing out the best in all of us,' and he took Anna by the arm and led her up through the choir stalls.

From the darkness at the rear of the little chapel to St Martin de Porres, Meehan watched, fascinated. Billy whispered, 'I said he was a nutter, didn't I? So how in the hell is he going to talk his way out of this one?'

'With his fingers, Billy, with his fingers,' Meehan said. 'I'd put a grand on it.' There was sincere admiration in his voice when he added. 'You know something. I'm enjoying every bleeding minute of this. It's always nice to see a real pro in action.' He sighed. 'There aren't many of us left.'

Fallon took off his trenchcoat and draped it over the back of a convenient choir stall. He sat down and adjusted the stool so that he could reach the pedals easily. Anna stood at his right hand.

'Have you tried leaving the trumpet in as I suggested?' he asked.

She nodded. 'It made quite a difference.'

'Good. I'll play something pretty solid and we'll see what else we can find wrong. What about the Bach Prelude and Fugue in D Major?'

'I only have it in Braille.'

'That's all right. I know it by heart.' He turned and looked down at Father da Costa and the two policemen on the other side of the altar rail. 'If you're interested, this is reputed to have been Albert Schweitzer's favourite piece.'

No one said a word. They stood there, waiting, and Fallon swung round to face the organ. It had been a long time – a hell of a long time and yet, quite suddenly and in some strange, incomprehensible way, it was only yesterday.

He prepared the swell organ, hands moving expertly – all stops except the Vox Humana and the Celeste and on the Great Organ, Diapasons and a four foot Principal.

He looked up at Anna gravely. 'As regards the Pedal Organ, I'd be disinclined to use any reed stops on this instrument. Only the sixteen-foot Diapason and the Bourdon and maybe a thirty-two-foot stop to give a good, solid tone. What do you think?'

She could not see the corner of his mouth lifted in a slight, sardonic smile and yet something of that smile was in his voice. She put a hand on his shoulder and said clearly, 'An interesting beginning, anyway.'

To her horror he said very softly, 'Why did you interfere?'

'Isn't that obvious?' she answered in a low voice. 'For Superintendent Miller and his inspector's sake. Now play.'

'God forgive you, but you're a terrible liar,' Fallon told her, and started.

He opened with a rising scale, not too fast, allowing each note to be heard, heeling and toeing with his left foot in a clear, bold, loud statement, playing with such astonishing power that Miller's wild surmise died on the instant for it was a masterly performance by any standard.

Father da Costa stood at the altar rail as if turned to stone, caught by the brilliance of Fallon's playing as he answered the opening statement with the chords of both hands on the sparkling Great Organ. He repeated, feet, then hands again, manual answering pedals until his left toe sounded the long four bar bottom A and his hands traced the brilliant passages announced by the pedals.

Miller tapped Father da Costa on the shoulder and whispered in his ear, 'Brilliant, but I'm running out of time, Father. Can we have our chat now?'

Father da Costa nodded reluctantly and led the way across to the sacristy. Fitzgerald was the last in and the door banged behind him in a sudden gust of wind.

Fallon stopped playing. 'Have they gone?' he asked softly.

Anna da Costa stared blindly down at him, a kind of awe on her face, reached out to touch his cheek. 'Who are you? she whispered. 'What are you?'

'A hell of a question to ask any man,' he said and, turning back to the organ, he moved into the opening passage again.

The music could be heard in the sacristy, muted yet throbbing through the old walls with a strange power. Father da Costa sat on the edge of the table.

'Cigarette, sir?' Fitzgerald produced an old, silver case. Father da Costa took one and the light that followed.

Miller observed him closely. The massive shoulders, that weathered, used-up face, the tangled grey beard, and suddenly realised with something close to annoyance that he actually liked the man. It was precisely for this reason that he decided to be as formal as possible.

'Well, Superintendent?' Father da Costa said.

'Have you changed your mind, sir, since we last spoke?'

'Not in the slightest.'

Miller fought hard to control his anger and Fitzgerald moved in smoothly. 'Have you been coerced in any way since this morning sir, or threatened?'

'Not at all, Inspector,' Father da Costa assured him with complete honesty.

'Does the name Meehan mean anything to you, sir?'

Father da Costa shook his head, frowning slightly, 'No, I don't think so. Should it?'

Miller nodded to Fitzgerald, who opened the briefcase he was carrying and produced a photo which he passed to the priest. 'Jack Meehan,' he said. 'Dandy Jack to his friends. That one was taken in London on the steps of West End Central police station after he was released for lack of evidence in an East End shooting last year.'

Meehan, wearing his usual double-breasted overcoat, smiled out at the world hugely, waving his hat in his right hand, his left arm encircling the shoulders of a well-known model girl.

'The girl is strictly for publicity purposes,' Fitzgerald said. 'In sexual matters his tastes run elsewhere. What you read on the sheet pinned to the back is all we have on him officially.'

Father da Costa read it with interest. Jack meehan was forty-eight and had joined the Royal Navy in 1943 at eighteen, serving on minesweepers until 1945 when he had been sentenced to a year's imprisonment and discharged with ignominy for breaking a Petty Officer's jaw in a brawl. In 1948 he had served six months on a minor smuggling charge and in 1954 a charge of conspiracy to rob the mails had been dropped for lack of evidence. Since then, he had been questioned by the police on over forty occasions in connection with indictable offences.

'You don't seem to be having much success,' Father da Costa said with a slight smile.

'There's nothing funny about Jack Meehan,' Miller said. 'In twenty-five years in the police force he's the nastiest thing I've ever come across. Remember the Kray brothers and the Richardson torture gang? Meehan's worse than the whole damn lot of them put together. He has an undertaking business here in the city, but behind that façade of respectability he heads an organisation that controls drug-pushing, prostitution, gambling and protection in most of the big cities in the north of England.'

'And you can't stop him? I find that surprising.'

'Rule by terror, Father. The Krays got away with it for years. Meehan makes them look like beginners. He's had men shot on many occasions – usually the kind of shotgun blast in the legs that doesn't kill, simply cripples. He likes them around as an advertisement.'

'You know this for a fact?'

'And couldn't prove it. Just as I couldn't

prove he was behind the worst case of organised child prostitution we ever had or that he disciplined one man by crucifying him with six-inch nails and another by making him eat his own excreta.'

For the briefest of moments, Father da Costa found himself back in that camp in North Korea – the first one where the softening up was mainly physical – lying half-dead in the latrine while a Chinese boot ground his face into a pile of human ordure. The guard had tried to make him eat, too, and he had refused, mainly because he thought he was dying anyway.

He pulled himself back to the present with an effort. 'And you think Meehan is behind the killing of Krasko this morning?'

'He has to be,' Miller told him. 'Krasko was, to put it politely, a business rival in every sense of the word. Meehan tried to take him under his wing and he refused. In Meehan's terms, he wouldn't see reason.'

'And a killer was brought in to execute him publicly?'

'To encourage the others,' Miller said. 'In

a sense, the very fact that Meehan dares to do such a thing is a measure of just how sick he is. He knows that I know he's behind the whole thing. But he wants me to know – wants everyone to know. He thinks nothing can touch him.'

Father da Costa looked down at the photo, frowning, and Fitzgerald said, 'We could get him this time, Father, with your help.'

Father da Costa shook his head, his face grave. 'I'm sorry, Inspector. I really am.'

Miller said in a harsh voice, 'Father da Costa, the only inference we can draw from your strange conduct is that you are aware of the identity of the man we are seeking. That you are in fact protecting him. Inspector Fitzgerald here, himself a Catholic, has suggested a possible explanation to me. That your knowledge is somehow bound up with the secrets of the confessional, if that is the term. Is there any truth in that supposition?'

'Believe me, Superintendent, if I could help you I would,' Father da Costa told him.

'You still refuse?'

'I'm afraid so.'

145

Miller glanced at his watch. 'All right, Father, I have an appointment in twenty minutes and I'd like you to come with me. No threats – no coercion. Just a simple request.'

'I see,' Father da Costa said. 'May I be permitted to ask where we are going?'

'To attend the post mortem of Janos Krasko at the city mortuary.'

'I see,' Father da Costa said. 'Tell me, Superintendent, is this supposed to be a challenge?'

'That's up to you, Father.'

Father da Costa stood up, suddenly weary. His will to resist was at a new low. He was sick of the whole wretched business. Strangely enough the only thing of which he was aware with any clarity was the sound of the organ, muted and far away.

'I have evening Mass, Superintendent, and supper at the refuge afterwards. I can't be long.'

'An hour at the most, sir, I'll have you brought back by car, but we really will have to leave now.'

146

Father da Costa opened the sacristy door and led the way back into the church. He paused at the altar, 'Anna?' he called.

Fallon stopped playing and the girl turned to face him. 'I'm just going out, my dear, with Superintendent Miller.'

'What about Mass?' she said.

'I won't be long. As for the organ,' he added, 'perhaps Mr Fallon would come back after Mass? We could discuss it then.'

'Glad to, Father,' Fallon called cheerfully.

Father da Costa, Miller and Inspector Fitzgerald walked down the aisle, past the chapel of St Martin de Porres, where Jack Meehan and his brother still sat in the shadows, and out of the front door.

It banged in the wind. There was silence. Fallon said softly, 'Well now, at a rough estimate, I'd say you've just saved my neck. I think he suspected something, the good Superintendent Miller.'

'But not now,' she said. 'Not after such playing. You were brilliant.'

He chuckled softly. 'That might have been true once, as I'll admit with becoming modesty, but not any more. My hands aren't what they were, for one thing.'

'Brilliant,' she said. 'There's no other word for it.'

She was genuinely moved and for the moment it was as if she had forgotten that other darker side. She groped for his hands, a smile on her face.

'As for your hands – what nonsense.' She took them in hers, still smiling, and then that smile was wiped clean. 'Your fingers?' she whispered, feeling at them. 'What happened?'

'Oh, those.' He pulled his hands free and examined the ugly, misshapen finger-ends. 'Some unfriends of mine pulled out my nails. A small matter on which we didn't quite see eye to eye.'

He stood up and pulled on his coat. She sat there, horror on her face and reached out a hand as if to touch him, pawing at space. He helped her to her feet and placed her coat about her shoulders.

'I don't understand,' she said.

'And please God, you never should,' he told her softly. 'Come on now and I'll take you home.'

They went down the altar steps and out through the sacristy. The door closed behind them. There was a moment of silence and then Billy Meehan stood up.

'Thank God for that. Can we kindly get the hell out of here now?'

'You can, not me,' Meehan told him. 'Find Fallon and stick to him like glue.'

'But I thought that was Varley's job?'

'So now I'm putting you on to it. Tell Varley to wait outside.'

'And what about you,' Billy said sullenly.

'Oh, I'll wait here for the priest to get back. Time we had a word.' He sighed and stretched his arms. 'I like it here. Nice and peaceful in the dark with all those candles flickering away there. Gives a fella time to think.' Billy hesitated as if trying to find some suitable reply and Meehan said irritably, 'Go on, piss off out of it for Christ's sake. I'll see you later.'

He leaned back, arms folded, and closed his eyes and Billy left by the front entrance to do as he was told.

* * *

149

It was raining hard in the cemetery. As they moved along the path to the presbytery, Fallon slipped her arm in his.

'Sometimes I think it's never going to stop,' she said. 'It's been like this for days.'

'I know,' he said.

They reached the front door, she opened it and paused in the porch while Fallon stood at the bottom of the steps looking up at her.

'Nothing seems to make sense to me any longer,' she said. 'I don't understand you or what's happened today or any part of it – not after hearing you play. It doesn't make sense. It doesn't fit.'

He smiled up at her gently. 'Go in now, girl dear, out of the cold. Stay safe in your own small world.'

'Not now,' she said. 'How can I? You've made me an accessory now, isn't that what they call it? I could have spoken up, but I didn't.'

It was the most terrible thing she could have said to him. He said hoarsely. 'Then why didn't you?'

'I gave my uncle my word, had you

forgotten? And I would not hurt him for worlds.'

Fallon moved back into the rain very softly, She called from the porch, 'Mr Fallon, are you there?'

He didn't reply. She stood there for a moment longer, uncertainty on her face, then went in and closed the door. Fallon turned and moved back along the path.

Billy had been watching them from the shelter of a large Victorian mausoleum, or rather, he had been watching Anna. She was different from the girls he was used to. Quiet, lady-like and yet she had an excellent figure. There was plenty of warmth beneath that cool exterior, he was certain of that, and the fact of her blindness made his stomach churn, exciting some perversity inside him and he got an almost instant erection.

Fallon paused, hands cupped to light a cigarette, and Billy drew back out of sight.

Fallon said, 'All right, Billy, I'm ready to go home now. Since you're here, you can drive me back to Jenny's place.'

Billy hesitated, then stepped reluctantly

into the open. 'Think you're bleeding smart, don't you?'

'To be smarter than you doesn't take much, sonny,' Fallon told him. 'And another thing. If I catch you hanging around here again, I'll be very annoyed.'

'Why don't you go stuff yourself,' Billy told him furiously.

He turned and walked rapidly towards the gate. Fallon was smiling as he went after him.

The city mortuary was built like a fort and encircled by twenty-foot walls of red brick to keep out prying eyes. When Miller's car reached the main entrance the driver got out and spoke into a voice box on the wall. He climbed back behind the wheel. A moment later the great steel gate slid back automatically and they passed into an inner courtyard.

'Here we are, Father,' Miller said. 'The most modern mortuary in Europe, or so they say.'

He and Fitzgerald got out first and Father

da Costa followed them. The inner building was all concrete and glass. Functional, but rather beautiful in its own way. They went up a concrete ramp to the rear entrance and a technician in white overalls opened the door for them.

'Good morning, Superintendent,' he said. 'Professor Lawlor said he'd meet you in the dressing-room. He's very anxious to get started.'

There was the constant low hum of the air-conditioning plant as they followed him along a maze of narrow corridors. Miller glanced over his shoulder at Father da Costa and said casually, 'They boast the purest air in the city up here. If you can breathe it at all, that is.'

It was the kind of remark that didn't seem to require an answer and Father da Costa made no attempt to make one. The technician opened a door, ushered them inside and left.

There were several washbasins, a shower in the corner, white hospital overalls and robes hanging on pegs on one wall. Underneath was a row of white rubber boots in various sizes. Miller and Fitzgerald removed their raincoats and the Superintendent took down a couple of white robes and passed one to Father da Costa.

'Here, put this on. You don't need to bother about boots.'

Father da Costa did as he was told and then the door opened and Professor Lawlor entered. 'Come on, Nick,' he said. 'You're holding me up.' And then he saw the priest and his eyes widened in surprise. 'Hello, Father.'

I'd like Father da Costa to observe, if you've no objection,' Miller said.

Professor Lawlor was wearing white overalls and boots and long pale-green rubber gloves, which he pulled at impatiently, 'As long as he doesn't get in the way. But do let's get on with it. I've got a lecture at the medical school at five.'

He led the way out and they followed along a short corridor and through a rubber swing door into the post mortem room. It was lit by fluorescent lighting so bright that it almost hurt the eyes and there was a row of half-a-dozen stainless steel operating tables.

Janos Krasko lay on his back on the one nearest the door, head raised on a wooden block. He was quite naked. Two technicians stood ready beside a trolley on which an assortment of surgical instruments was laid out neatly. The greatest surprise for Father da Costa were the closed circuit television cameras, one set close up to the operating table, the other waiting nearby on a movable trolley.

'As you can see, Father, science marches on,' Miller said. 'These days in a case like this everything's videotaped and in colour.'

'Is that necessary?' Father da Costa asked him.

'It certainly is. Especially when you get the kind of defence council who hasn't got much to go on and tries bringing in his own expert witness. In other words, some other eminent pathologist with his own particular theory about what happened.'

One of the technicians was fastening a throat mike around Lawlor's throat and

Miller nodded. 'The medical profession are great on opinions, Father, I've learned that the hard way.'

Lawlor smiled frostily. 'Don't get bitter in your old age, Nick. Have you witnessed a post mortem before, Father?'

'Not in your terms, Professor.'

'I see. Well, if you feel sick, you know where the dressing-room is and please stand well back – all of you.' He turned and addressed the camera men and technicians. 'Right, gentlemen, let's get started.'

It should have been like something out of a nightmare. That it wasn't was probably due to Lawlor as much as anything else. That and the general atmosphere of clinical efficiency.

He was really quite brilliant. More than competent in every department. An artist with a knife who kept up a running commentary in that dry, precise voice of his during the entire proceedings.

'Everything he says is recorded,' Miller whispered. 'To go with the video.'

Father da Costa watched, fascinated, as Lawlor drew a scalpel around the skull. He grasped the hair firmly and pulled the entire face forward, eyeballs and all, like a crumpled rubber mask.

He nodded to the technicians who handed him a small electric saw and switched on. Lawlor began to cut round the top of the skull very carefully.

'They call it a de Soutter,' Miller whispered again. 'Works on a vibratory principle. A circular saw would cut too quickly.'

There was very little smell, everything being drawn up by extractor fans in the ceiling above the table. Lawlor switched off the saw and handed it to the technician. He lifted off the neat skullcap of bone and placed it on the table, then carefully removed the brain and put it in a rather commonplace red, plastic basin which one of the technicians held ready.

The technician carried it across to the sink and Lawlor weighed it carefully. He said to Miller, 'I'll leave my examination of this until I've finished going through the motions on the rest of him. All right?'

'Fine,' Miller said.

Lawlor returned to the corpse, picked up a large scalpel and opened the entire body from throat to belly. There was virtually no blood, only a deep layer of yellow fat, red meat underneath. He opened the body up like an old overcoat, working fast and efficiently, never stopping for a moment.

Father da Costa said, 'Is this necessary? The wound was in the head. We know that.'

The Coroner will demand a report that is complete in every detail,' Miller told him. 'That's what the law says he's entitled to and that's what he expects. It's not as cruel as you think. We had a case the other year. An old man found dead at his home. Apparent heart failure. When Lawlor opened him up he was able to confirm that, and if he'd stopped at the heart that would have been the end of the matter.'

'There was more?'

'Fractured vertebrae somewhere in the neck area. I forget the details, but it meant that the old boy had been roughly handled by someone, which led us to a character who'd been making a nuisance of himself preying on old people. The sort who knocks on the door, insists he was told to clean the drains and demands ten quid.'

'What happened to him?'

'The court accepted a plea of manslaughter. Gave him five years so he's due out soon. A crazy world, Father.'

'And what would you have done with him?'

'I'd have hung him,' Miller said simply. 'You see, for me, it's a state of war now. A question of survival. Liberal principles are all very fine as long as they leave you with something to have principles about.'

Which made sense in its own way and it was hard to argue. Father da Costa moved to one side as the technicians carried the various organs across to the sink in more plastic basins. Each item was weighed, then passed to Lawlor who sliced it quickly into sections on a wooden block with a large knife. Heart, lungs, liver, kidneys, intestines – they all received the same treatment with astonishing speed and the camera on the trolley recorded everything at his side.

Finally he was finished and put down his knife. 'That's it,' he said to Miller. 'Nothing worth mentioning. I'll go to town on the brain after I've had a cigarette.' He smiled at da Costa,

'Well, what did you think?'

'An extraordinary experience,' Father da Costa said. 'Disquieting more than anything else.'

'To find that man is just so much raw meat?' Professor Lawlor said.

'Is that what you think?'

'See for yourself.'

Lawlor crossed to the operating table, and Father da Costa went with him. The body was open to the view and quite empty. Gutted. Nothing but space from inside the rib cage and down into the penis.

'Remember that poem of Eliot's The Hollow Men? Well, this is what he was getting at or so it's always seemed to me.'

'And you think that's all there is?'

'Don't you?' Lawlor demanded.

One of the technicians replaced the skullcap of bone and pulled the scalp back

into place. Amazing how easily the face settled
into position again. Quite remarkable.

Father da Costa said, 'A superb piece of
engineering, the human body. Infinitely functional. There seems to be no task that a man
cannot cope with if he so desires. Wouldn't
you agree, Professor?'

'I suppose so.'

'Sometimes I find the mystery of it quite
terrifying. I mean, is this all that's left in the
end of an Einstein, let's say, or a Picasso? A
gutted body, a few scraps of raw meat swilling
about in the bottom of a plastic bucket?'

'Ah no you don't.' Lawlor grinned tiredly.
'No metaphysics, if you please, Father, I've
got other things to do.' He turned to Miller.
'Have you seen enough?'

'I think so,' Miller said.

'Good, then get this devil's advocate out
of here and leave me in peace to finish. It
will be the morning before you get the full
report now.' He grinned at Father da Costa
again. 'I won't shake hands for obvious
reasons, but any time you're passing just drop
in. There's always someone here.'

He laughed at his own joke, was still laughing when they went back to the dressing-room. One of the technicians went with them to make sure that the robes they had worn went straight into the dirty laundry basket, so there was no opportunity to talk.

Miller led the way back outside, feeling tired and depressed. He had lost, he knew that already. The trouble was he didn't really know what to do next, except to take the kind of official action he'd been hoping to avoid.

It was still raining when they went out into the courtyard. When they reached the car, Fitzgerald opened the door and Father da Costa climbed in. Miller followed him. Fitzgerald sat in the front with the driver.

As they moved out into the city traffic, Miller said, 'I wanted you to see the reality of it and it hasn't made the slightest difference, has it?'

Father da Costa said, 'When I was twenty years of age, I dropped into the Cretan mountains by parachute, dressed as a peasant. All very romantic. Action by night

162

– that sort of thing. When I arrived at the local village inn I was arrested at gunpoint by a German undercover agent. A member of the Feldgendarmerie.'

Miller was interested in spite of himself. 'You'd been betrayed?'

'Something like that. He wasn't a bad sort. Told me he was sorry, but that he'd have to hold me till the Gestapo got there. We had a drink together. I managed to hit him on the head with a wine bottle.'

Father da Costa stared back into the past and Miller said gently. 'What happened?'

'He shot me in the left lung and I choked him to death with my bare hands.' Father da Costa held them up. 'I've prayed for him every day of my life since.'

They turned into the street at the side of the church and Miller said wearily, 'All right, I get the picture.' The car pulled in at the kerb and there was a new formality in his voice when he said, 'In legal terms, your attitude in this matter makes you an accessory after the fact. You understand that?'

'Perfectly,' da Costa told him.

'All right,' Miller said. 'This is what I intend to do. I shall approach your superior in a final effort to make you see sense.'

'Monsignor O'Halloran is the man you want. I tried to see him myself earlier, but he's out of town. He'll be back in the morning – but it won't do you any good.'

'Then I'll apply to the Director of Public Prosecutions for a warrant for your arrest.'

Father da Costa nodded soberly. 'You must do what you think is right. I see that, Superintendent.' He opened the door and got out. 'I'll pray for you.'

'Pray for me!' Miller ground his teeth together as the car moved away. 'Have you ever heard the like?'

'I know, sir,' Fitzgerald said. 'He's quite a man, isn't he?'

It was cold in the church and damp as Father da Costa opened the door and moved inside. Not long till Mass. He felt tired – wretchedly tired. It had been an awful day – the worst he could remember in a great many years

– since the Chinese prison camp at Chong Sam. If only Fallon and Miller – all of them – would simply fade away, cease to exist.

He dipped his fingers in the Holy Water and on his right a match flared in the darkness of the little side chapel to St Martin de Porres as someone lit a candle, illuminating a familiar face.

There was a slight pause and then the Devil moved out of the darkness and Father da Costa girded up his loins to meet him.

8

The Devil and all his Works

'What do you want here, Mr Meehan?' Father da Costa said.

'You know who I am?'

'Oh, yes,' Father da Costa told him. 'I was taught to recognise the Devil from a very early age.'

Meehan stared at him for a moment in genuine amazement and then he laughed harshly, his head thrown back, and the sound echoed up into the rafters.

'That's good. I like that.' Father da Costa said nothing and Meehan shrugged and turned to look down towards the altar. 'I used to come here when I was a kid. I was an acolyte.' He turned and there was a challenge in his voice. 'You don't believe me?'

'Shouldn't I?'

Meehan nodded towards the altar. 'I've stood up there many a time when it was my turn to serve at Mass. Scarlet cassock, white cotta. My old lady used to launder them every week. She loved seeing me up there. Father O'Malley was the priest in those days.'

'I've heard of him,' Father da Costa said.

'Tough as old boots.' Meehan was warming to his theme now – enjoying himself. 'I remember one Saturday evening, a couple of drunken Micks came in just before Mass and started turning things upside down. Duffed them up proper, he did. Straight out on their ear. Said they'd desecrated God's house and all that stuff.' He shook his head. 'A real old sod, he was. He once caught me with a packet of fags I'd nicked from a shop round the corner. Didn't call the law. Just took a stick to me in the sacristy.' He chuckled. 'Kept me honest for a fortnight that, Father. Straight up.'

Father da Costa said quietly, 'What do you want here, Mr Meehan?'

Meehan made a sweeping gesture with one arm that took in the whole church. 'Not what it was, I can tell you. Used to be beautiful, a real picture, but now . . .' He shrugged. 'Ready to fall down any time. This restoration fund of yours? I hear you've not been getting very far.'

Father da Costa saw it all. 'And you'd like to help, is that it?'

'That's it, Father, that's it exactly.'

The door opened behind them, they both turned and saw an old lady with a shopping-bag enter. As she genuflected, Father da Costa said, 'We can't talk here. Come with me.'

They went up in the hoist to the top of the tower. It was still raining as he led the way out along the catwalk, but the mist had lifted and the view of the city was remarkable. In the far distance, perhaps four or five miles away, it was even possible to see the edge of the moors smudging the grey sky.

Meehan was genuinely delighted, 'Heh, I was up here once when I was a kid. Inside the belfry. It was different then.' He leaned over the rail and pointed to where the bulldozers were excavating in the brickfield. 'We used to live there. Thirteen, Khyber Street.'

He turned to Father da Costa who made no reply. Meehan said softly, 'This arrangement between you and Fallon? You going to stick to it?'

Father da Costa said, 'What arrangement would that be?'

'Come off it,' Meehan replied impatiently. 'This confession thing. I know all about it. He told me.'

'Then, as a Catholic yourself, you must know that there is nothing I can say. The secrets of the confessional are absolute.'

Meehan laughed harshly, 'I know. He's got brains, that Fallon. He shut you up good, didn't he?'

A small, hot spark of anger moved in Father da Costa and he breathed deeply to control it. 'If you say so.'

Meehan chuckled. 'Never mind, Father, I always pay my debts. How much?' His gesture took in the church, the scaffolding, everything. 'To put all this right?'

'Fifteen thousand pounds,' Father da Costa

told him. 'For essential preliminary work. More would be needed later.'

'Easy,' Meehan said. 'With my help you could pick that up inside two or three months.'

'Might I ask how?'

Meehan lit a cigarette. 'For a start, there's the clubs. Dozens of them all over the north. They'll all put the old collecting-box round if I give the word.'

'And you actually imagine that I could take it?'

Meehan looked genuinely bewildered. 'It's only money, isn't it? Pieces of paper. A medium of exchange, that's what the bright boys call it. Isn't that what you need?'

'In case you've forgotten, Mr Meehan, Christ drove the money-lenders *out* of the temple. He didn't ask them for a contribution to the cause.'

Meehan frowned. 'I don't get it.'

'Then let me put it this way. My religion teaches me that reconciliation with God is always possible. That no human being, however degraded or evil, is beyond God's mercy. I had always believed that until now.'

Meehan's face was pale with fury. He grabbed da Costa's arm and pushed him towards the rail, pointing down at the brickfield.

'Thirteen, Khyber Street. A back-to-back rabbit hutch. One room downstairs, two up. One stinking lavatory to every four houses. My old man cleared off when I was a kid – he had sense. My old lady – she kept us going by cleaning when she could get it. When she couldn't,there were always ten bob quickies behind the boozer on a Saturday night. A bloody whore, that's all she was.'

'Who found time to clean and iron your cassock and cotta each week?' Father da Costa said. 'Who fed you and washed you and sent you to this church?'

'To hell with that,' Meehan said wildly. 'All she ever got – all anybody from Khyber Street ever got – was screwed into the ground, but not me. Not Jack Meehan. I'm up here now. I'm on top of the world where nobody can touch me.'

Father da Costa felt no pity, only a terrible

disgust. He said calmly, 'I believe you to be the most evil and perverted creature it has ever been my misfortune to meet. If I could, I would hand you over to the proper authorities gladly. Tell them everything, but for reasons well known to you, this is impossible.'

Meehan seemed to be more in control of himself again. He said, with a sneer, 'That's good, that is. Me, you wouldn't touch with a ten-foot pole, but Fallon, he's different, isn't he? I mean, he only murders women and children.'

For a moment, Father da Costa had to fight for breath. When he spoke, it was with difficulty, 'What are you talking about?

'Don't say he hasn't told you,' Meehan jeered. 'Nothing about Belfast or Londonderry or that bus full of schoolkids he blew up?' He leaned forward, a strange intent look on his face and then he smiled, softly 'You don't like that, do you? Fell for his Irish charm. Did you fancy him, then? I've heard some of you priests . . .'

There was a hand at his throat, a hand of

iron and he was back against the cage of the hoist, fighting for his very life, the priest's eyes sparking fire. Meehan tried to bring up a knee and found only a thigh turned expertly to block it. Father da Costa shook him like a rat, then opened the door and threw him inside.

The cage door slammed as Meehan picked himself up. 'I'll have you for this,' he said hoarsely. 'You're dead meat.'

'My God, Mr Meehan,' Father da Costa said softly through the bars of the cage, 'is a God of Love. But he is also a God of Wrath. I leave you in his hands.'

He pressed the button and the cage started to descend.

As Meehan emerged from the church porch, a sudden flurry of wind dashed rain in his face. He turned up his collar and paused to light a cigarette. It was beginning to get dark and as he went down the steps he noticed a number of men waiting by a side door, sheltering against the wall from the rain.

Human derelicts, most of them, in tattered coats and broken boots.

He moved across the street and Varley came out of the doorway of the old warehouse on the corner. 'I waited, Mr Meehan, like Billy said.'

'What happened to Fallon?'

'Went off in the car with Billy.'

Meehan frowned, but for the moment, that could wait and he turned his attention to the queue again. 'What are they all waiting for? This bleeding soup kitchen to open?'

'That's right, Mr Meehan. In the crypt.'

Meehan stared across at the queue for a while and then smiled suddenly. He opened his wallet and extracted a bundle of one-pound notes.

'I make it twenty-two in that queue, Charlie. You give them a quid apiece with my compliments and tell them the pub on the corner's just opened.'

Varley, mystified, crossed the street to distribute his largesse and within seconds, the queue was breaking up, several of the men touching their caps to Meehan who nodded cheerfully as they shuffled past. When Varley came back, there was no one left outside the door.

'He's going to have a lot of bleeding soup on his hands tonight,' Meehan said, grinning.

'I don't know about that, Mr Meehan,' Varley pointed out. 'They'll only come back when they've spent up.'

'And by then they'll have a skinful, won't they, so they might give him a little trouble. In fact, I think we'll make sure they do. Get hold of that bouncer from the Kit Kat Club. The Irishman, O'Hara.'

'Big Mick, Mr Meehan?' Varley stirred uneasily. 'I'm not too happy about that. He's a terrible man when he gets going.'

Meehan knocked off his cap and grabbed him by the hair. 'You tell him to be outside that door with one of his mates at opening time. Nobody goes in for the first hour. Nobody. He waits for at least a dozen drunks to back him, then he goes in and smashes the place up. If he does it right, it's worth twenty-five quid. If the priest breaks an arm, accidental like, it's worth fifty.'

Varley scrambled for his cap in the gutter.
'Is that all, Mr Meehan?' he asked fearfully.

'It'll do for starters.' Meehan was chuck-
ling to himself as he walked away.

Father da Costa could count on only three
acolytes for evening Mass. The parish was
dying, that was the trouble. As the houses
came down, the people moved away to the
new estates, leaving only the office blocks.
It was a hopeless task, he had known that
when they sent him to Holy Name. His
superiors had known. A hopeless task to
teach him humility, wasn't that what the
bishop had said? A little humility for a man
who had been arrogant enough to think he
could change the world. Remake the Church
in his own image.

Two of the boys were West Indians, the
other English of Hungarian parents. All a
product of the few slum streets still remaining.
They stood in the corner waiting for him,
whispering together, occasionally laughing,
newly-washed, hair combed, bright in their

scarlet cassocks and white cottas. Had Jack Meehan looked like that once?

The memory was like a sword in the heart. The fact of his own violence, the killing rage. The violence that had been so often his undoing through the years. The men he had killed in the war – that was one thing, but after . . . the Chinese soldier in Korea machine-gunning a column of refugees. He had picked up a rifle and shot the man through the head at two hundred yards. Expertly, skilfully, the old soldier temporarily in control. Had he been wrong? Had it really been wrong when so many lives had been saved? And that Portuguese Captain in Mozambique stringing up guerrillas by their ankles. He had beaten the man half to death, the incident that had finally sent him home in disgrace.

'The days when bishops rode into battle with a mace in one hand are over, my friend.' The Bishop's voice echoed faintly 'Your task is to save souls.'

Violence for Violence. That was Meehan's way. Sick and disgusted, Father da Costa took off the violet stole he had worn for confession and put on a green one, crossing it under his girdle to represent Christ's passion and death. As he put on an old rose-coloured cope, the outer door opened and Anna came in, her stick in one hand, a raincoat over her.

He moved to take the raincoat, holding her shoulders briefly. 'Are you all right?'

She turned at once, concern on her face. 'What is it? You're upset. Has anything happened?'

'I had an unpleasant interview with the man Meehan,' he replied in a low voice. 'He said certain things concerning Fallon. Things which could explain a great deal. I'll tell you later.'

She frowned slightly, but he led her to the door and opened it, pushing her through into the church. He waited for a few moments to give her time to reach the organ, then nodded to the boys. They formed into their tiny procession, one of them opening the door, and as the organ started to play, they moved into the church.

It was a place of shadows, candlelight and

darkness alternating, cold and damp. There were perhaps fifteen people in the congregation, no more. He had never felt so dispirited, so close to the final edge of things, not since Korea, and then he looked across at the figure of the Virgin. She seemed to float there in the candlelight, so calm, so serene and the slight half-smile on the parted lips seemed somehow for him alone.

'*Asperges me*,' he intoned and moved down the aisle, one of the West Indian boys carrying the bucket of holy water in front of him, Father da Costa sprinkling the heads of his congregation as he passed, symbolically washing them clean.

'And who will cleanse me?' he asked himself desperately. 'Who?'

In the faded rose cope, hands together, he commenced the mass. 'I confess to Almighty God, and to you, my brothers and sisters, that I have sinned through my own fault,' Here, he struck his breast once as ritual required. 'In my thoughts and in my words, in what I have done, and in what I have failed to do.'

The voices of the congregation swelled up in unison behind him. There were tears on his face, the first in many years, and he struck his breast again.

'Lord, have mercy on me,' he whispered. 'Help me. Show me what to do.'

9

The Executioner

The wind howled through the city like a living thing, driving rain before it, clearing the streets, rattling old window frames, tapping at the glass like some invisible presence.

When Billy Meehan went into Jenny Fox's bedroom, she was standing in front of the mirror combing her hair. She was wearing the black pleated mini skirt, dark stockings, patent-leather, high-heeled shoes and a white blouse. She looked extremely attractive.

As she turned, Billy closed the door and said softly, 'Nice, very nice. He's still in his room, isn't he?'

'He said he was going out again, though.'

'We'll have to change his mind then, won't

we?' Billy went and sat on the bed. 'Come here.'

She fought to control the instant panic that threatened to choke her, the disgust that made her flesh crawl as she moved towards him.

He slipped his hands under her skirt, fondling the warm flesh at the top of the stockings. 'That's a good girl. He'll like that. They always do.' He stared up at her, that strange, dreamy look in his eyes again. 'You muck this up for me, you'll be in trouble. I mean, I'd have to punish you and you wouldn't like that, would you?'

Her heart thudded painfully, 'Please, Billy! Please!'

'Then do it right. I want to see what makes this guy tick.'

He pushed her away, got up and moved to a small picture on the wall. He removed it carefully. There was a tiny peephole underneath, skilfully placed and he peered through.

After a few moments, he turned and nodded. 'Just taken his shirt off. Now you get in there and remember – I'll be watching.'

His mouth was slack, his hands trembling a little and she turned, choking back her disgust, opened the door and slipped outside.

Fallon was standing at the washbasin, stripped to the waist, lather on his face, when she knocked on the door and went in. He turned to greet her, a bone-handled cut-throat razor in one hand.

She leaned against the door. 'Sorry about the razor. It was all I could find.'

'That's all right.' He smiled. 'My father had one of these. Wouldn't use anything else till the day he died.'

A line of ugly, puckered scars cut across his abdomen down into the left hip. Her eyes widened. 'What happened?'

He glanced down. 'Oh, that – a machine-gun burst. One of those times I should have moved faster than I did.'

'Were you in the army?'

'In a manner of speaking.'

He turned back to the mirror to finish shaving. She moved across and stood beside

183

him. He smiled sideways, crookedly, stretching his mouth for the razor.

'You look nice enough to eat. Going somewhere?'

There was that warmth again, that pricking behind her eyes and she suddenly realised, with a sense of wonder, just how much she had come to like this strange, small man, and in the same moment remembered Billy watching her every move on the other side of that damned wall.

She smiled archly and ran a finger down his bare arm. 'I thought I might stay in tonight. What about you?'

Fallon's eyes flickered towards her once, something close to amusement in them. 'Girl dear, you don't know what you'd be getting into. And me twice your age.'

'I've got a bottle of Irish whiskey in.'

'God save us and isn't that enough to tempt the Devil himself?'

He continued his shaving and she moved across to the bed and sat down. It wasn't going right – it wasn't going right at all and at the thought of Billy's anger, she turned cold inside. She summoned up all her resources and tried again.

'Mind if I have a cigarette?'

There was a packet on the bedside table and a box of matches. She took one, lit it and leaned back on the bed, a pillow behind her shoulders.

'Have you really got to go out?'

She raised one knee so that the skirt slid back provocatively exposing bare flesh at the top of dark stockings, sheer black nylon briefs.

Fallon sighed heavily, put down the razor and picked up a towel. He wiped the foam from his face as he crossed to the bed and stood looking down at her.

'You'll catch cold.' He smiled softly and pulled down her skirt. 'If you're not careful. And I'm still going out, but I'll have a glass with you before I do, so be off now and open the bottle.'

He pulled her up from the bed and pushed her firmly across the room. She turned at the door, fear in her eyes. 'Please?' she said fiercely. 'Please?'

He frowned slightly and then a brief, sad

smile touched his mouth. He kissed her gently on the lips and shook his head. 'Not me, girl dear, not me in the whole wide world. You need a man . . . I'm just a corpse walking.'

It was such a terrible remark, so dreadful in its implication, that for the moment it drove every other thought from her mind. She stared up at him, eyes wide, and he opened the door and pushed her outside.

Fear possessed her now, such fear as she had never known. She couldn't face what awaited her in her bedroom. If she could only get downstairs – but it was already too late for as she tiptoed past, the door opened and Billy pulled her so violently into the bedroom that she stumbled, losing a shoe and went sprawling across the bed.

She turned fearfully and found him already unbuckling his belt. 'You cocked it up, didn't you?' he said softly. 'And after all I've done for you.'

'Please, Billy. Please don't,' she said. 'I'll do anything.'

'You can say that again. You're going to get one of my specials, just to keep you in line, and maybe next time I tell you to do something, you'll bloody well make sure it gets done.' He started to unfasten his trousers. 'Go on, turn over.' She was almost choking and shook her head dumbly. His face was like a mirror breaking, madness staring at her from those pale eyes and he struck her heavily across the face.

'You do as you're bloody well told, you bitch.'

He grabbed her by the hair, forcing her round until she sprawled across the edge of the bed, face down. His other hand tore at her briefs, pulling them down, And then, as she felt his hardness, as he forced himself between her buttocks like some animal, she screamed at the top of her voice, head arched back in agony.

The door opened so violently that it splintered against the wall and Fallon stood there, one side of his face still lathered, the cut-throat razor open in his right hand.

187

Billy turned from the girl, mouthing incoherently, clutching at his trousers, and as he stood up Fallon took two quick paces into the room and kicked him in the privates. Billy went down like a stone and lay there twitching, knees drawn up to his chest in a foetal position.

The girl adjusted her clothes as best she could and got up, every last shred of decency stripped from her, tears pouring down her face. Fallon wiped lather from his cheek mechanically with the back of his hand and his eyes were very dark.

She could hardly speak for sobbing. 'He made me go into your room tonight. He was watching.'

She gestured towards the wall and Fallon crossed to the peephole. He turned slowly. 'Does this kind of thing happen often?'

'He likes to watch.'

'And you? What about you?'

'I'm a whore,' she said and suddenly it erupted from her. All the disgust, the self-hate, born of years of degradation. 'Have you any idea what that means? He started me early, his brother.'

188

'Jack Meehan?'

'Who else? I was thirteen. Just right for a certain kind of client, and from then on it's been downhill all the way.'

'You could leave?'

'Where would I go to?' She had regained some of her composure now. 'It takes money. And I have a three-year-old daughter to think of.'

'Here – in this place?'

She shook her head. 'I board her out with a woman. A nice woman in a decent part of town, but Billy knows where she is.'

At that moment he stirred and pushed himself up on one elbow. There were tears in his eyes and his mouth was flecked with foam.

'You've had it,' he said faintly. 'When my brother hears about this you're a dead man.'

He started to zip up his trousers and Fallon crouched down beside him. 'My grandfather,' he began in a conversational tone, 'kept a farm back home in Ireland. Sheep mostly. And every year, he'd geld a few to improve the flavour of the mutton or make the wool grow more – something like that. Do you know what geld means, Billy boy?'

'Like hell I do. You're crackers,' Billy said angrily. 'Like all the bloody Irish.'

'It means he cut off their balls with a pair of sheep shears.'

An expression of frozen horror appeared on the boy's face and Fallon said softly, 'Touch this girl in any way from now on,' he held up the cut-throat razor, 'and I will attend to you personally. My word on it.'

The boy scrambled away from him and pushed himself up against the wall, clutching at his trousers. 'You're mad,' he whispered. 'Raving mad.'

'That's it, Billy,' Fallon said. 'Capable of anything and don't you forget it.'

The boy ducked out through the open door, his feet thundered on the stairs. The front door banged.

Fallon turned, a hand to his cheek. 'Could I finish my shaving now, do you suppose?'

She ran forward, gripping his arms fiercely. 'Please don't go out. Please don't leave me.'

'I must,' he said. 'He won't be back, not as long as I'm staying here.'

'And afterwards?'

'We'll think of something.'

She turned away and he grabbed her hand quickly. 'I'll be an hour, no more, I promise, and then we can have that glass of whiskey. How's that?'

She turned, peering at him uncertainly. The tears had streaked her make-up, making her somehow seem very young. 'You mean it?'

'On the word of an Irish gentleman.'

She flung her arms about his neck in delight. 'Oh. I'll be good to you. I really will.'

He put a finger on her mouth. 'There's no need. No need at all.' He patted her cheek. 'I'll be back, I promise. Only do one thing for me.'

'What's that?'

'Wash your face, for God's sake.'

He closed the door gently as he went out and she moved across to the washbasin and looked into the mirror. He was right. She looked terrible and yet for the first time in years, the eyes were smiling. Smiling through that streaked whore's mask. She picked up a flannel and some soap and started to wash her face thoroughly.

Father da Costa couldn't understand it. The refuge had been open for just over an hour without a single customer. In all the months he had been operating from the old crypt he had never known such a thing.

It wasn't much of a place, but the stone walls had been neatly whitewashed, there was a coke fire in the stove, benches and trestle tables. Anna sat behind one of them, knitting a sweater. The soup was in front of her in a heat-retaining container, plates piled beside it. There were several loaves of yesterday's bread supplied free by arrangement with a local bakery.

Father da Costa put more coke on the stove and stirred it impatiently with the poker. Anna stopped knitting. 'What do you think has happened?'

'God knows,' he said. 'I'm sure I don't.' He walked to the door and went out to the porch.

The street was apparently deserted. The rain had declined into a light drizzle. He went back inside.

The Irishman, O'Hara, the one Varley had referred to as Big Mick, moved out of the entrance to a small yard halfway up the street and stood under a lamp. He was a tall, broad-shouldered man, six foot three or four at least, with curling, black hair and a perpetual smile. The man who moved out of the shadows to join him was two or three inches shorter and had a broken nose.

It was at this moment that Fallon turned into the end of the street. He approached silently, pausing in the darkness to take stock of the situation when he saw O'Hara and his friend. When the Irishman started speaking. Fallon moved into a convenient doorway and listened.

'Sure and I think the reverend gentleman's just about ready for it, Daniel,' O'Hara said. 'How many have we got in there now?'

Daniel snapped his fingers and several shadowy figures emerged from the darkness. He counted them quickly. 'I make it eight,' he said. 'That's ten including us.'

'Nine,' O'Hara said. 'You stay outside and watch the door, just in case. They all know what to do?'

'I've seen to that,' Daniel said. 'For a quid apiece they'll take the place apart.'

O'Hara turned to address the shadowy group. 'Remember one thing. Da Costa – he's mine.'

Daniel said, 'Doesn't that worry you, Mick? I mean you being an Irishman and so on. After all, he's a priest.'

'I've a terrible confession to make, Daniel.' O'Hara put a hand on his shoulder. 'Some Irishmen are Protestants and I'm one of them.' He turned to the others. 'Come on, lads,' he said and crossed the road.

They went in through the door and Daniel waited by the railings, his ear cocked for the first sound of a disturbance from inside. There was a slight, polite cough from behind and when he turned, Fallon was standing a yard or two away, hands in pockets.

'Where in hell did you spring from?' Daniel demanded. 'Never mind that,' Fallon said. 'What's going on in there?'

Daniel knew trouble when he saw it, but completely miscalculated his man. 'You little squirt,' he said contemptuously. 'Get the hell out of it.'

He moved in fast, his hands reaching out to destroy, but they only fastened on thin air as his feet were kicked expertly from beneath him.

He thudded against the wet pavement and scrambled to his feet, mouthing obscenities. Fallon seized his right wrist with both hands, twisting it up and around. Daniel gave a cry of agony as the muscle started to give. Still keeping that terrible hold in position, Fallon ran him headfirst into the railings.

Daniel pulled himself up off his knees, blood on his face, one hand out in supplication. 'No more, for Christ's sake.'

'All right,' Fallon said. 'Answers then. What's the game?'

'They're supposed to turn the place over.'

'Who for?' Daniel hesitated and Fallon kicked his feet from under him. 'Who for?'

'Jack Meehan,' Daniel gabbled.

Fallon pulled him to his feet and stood back.

195

'Next time you get a bullet in the kneecap. That's a promise. Now get out of it.'

Daniel turned and staggered into the darkness.

At the first sudden noisy rush, Father da Costa knew he was in trouble. As he moved forward, a bench went over and then another. Hands pawed at him, someone pulled his cassock. He was aware of Anna crying out in alarm and turning, saw O'Hara grab her from behind, arms about her waist.

'Now then, darlin', what about a little kiss?' he demanded.

She pulled away from him in a panic, hands reaching out blindly and cannoned into the trestle table, knocking it over, soup spilling out across the floor, plates clattering.

As Father da Costa fought to get towards her, O'Hara laughed out loud. 'Now look what you've done.'

A soft, quiet voice called from the doorway, cutting through the noise.

'Mickeen O'Hara. Is it you I see?'

The room went quiet. Everyone waited. O'Hara turned, an expression of disbelief on his face that seemed to say this couldn't be happening. The expression was quickly replaced by one that was a mixture of awe and fear.

'God in heaven,' he whispered. 'Is that you, Martin?'

Fallon went towards him, hands in pockets and everyone waited. He said softly, 'Tell them to clean the place up, Mick, like a good boy, then wait for me outside.'

O'Hara did as he was told without hesitation and moved towards the door. The other men started to right the tables and benches, one of them got a bucket and mop and started on the floor.

Father da Costa had moved to comfort Anna and Fallon joined them. 'I'm sorry about that, Father,' he said. 'It won't happen again.'

'Meehan?' Father da Costa asked.

Fallon nodded. 'Were you expecting something like this?'

'He came to see me earlier this evening.

197

You might say we didn't get on too well.' He hesitated. 'The big Irishman. He knew you.'

'Little friend of all the world, that's me.' Fallon smiled. 'Good night to you,' he said and turned to the door.

Father da Costa reached him as he opened it and put a hand on his arm. 'We must talk, Fallon. You owe me that.'

'All right,' Fallon said. 'When?'

'I'll be busy in the morning, but I don't have a lunchtime confession tomorrow. Will one o'clock suit you? At the presbytery.'

'I'll be there.'

Fallon went out, closing the door behind him and crossed the street to where O'Hara waited nervously under the lamp. As Fallon approached he turned to face him.

'Before God, if I'd known you were mixed up in this, Martin I wouldn't have come within a mile of it. I thought you were dead by now – we all did.'

'All right,' Fallon said. 'How much was Meehan paying you?'

'Twenty-five quid. Fifty if the priest got a broken arm.'

'How much in advance?'

'Not a sou.'

Fallon opened his wallet, took out two ten-pound notes and handed them to him. 'Travelling money – for old times' sake. I don't think it's going to be too healthy for you round here. Not when Jack Meehan finds out you've let him down.'

'God bless you, Martin, I'll be out of it this very night.' He started to turn away, then hesitated. 'Does it bother you any more, Martin, what happened back there?'

'Every minute of every hour of every day of my life,' Fallon said with deep conviction and he turned and walked away up the side street.

From the shelter of the porch, Father da Costa saw O'Hara cross the main road. He made for the pub on the corner, going in at the saloon bar entrance and Father da Costa went after him.

It was quiet in the saloon bar which was why O'Hara had chosen it. He was still badly shaken and ordered a large whisky which he swallowed at once. As he asked for another, the door opened and Father da Costa entered.

O'Hara tried to brazen it out. 'So there you are, Father,' he said. 'Will you have a drink with me?'

'I'd sooner drink with the Devil.' Father da Costa dragged him across to a nearby booth and sat opposite him. 'Where did you know Fallon?' he demanded. 'Before tonight, I mean?'

O'Hara stared at him in blank astonishment, glass half-raised to his lips. 'Fallon?' he said. 'I don't know anyone called Fallon.'

'Martin Fallon, you fool,' Father da Costa said impatiently. 'Haven't I just seen you talking together outside the church?'

'Oh, you mean Martin,' O'Hara said. 'Fallon – is that what he's calling himself now?'

'What can you tell me about him?'

'Why should I tell you anything?'

'Because I'll ring for the police and put you in charge for assault if you don't. Detective-Superintendent Miller is a personal friend. He'll be happy to oblige, I'm sure.'

'All right, Father, you can call off the dogs.' O'Hara, mellowed by two large whiskies, went to the bar for a third and returned. 'What do you want to know for?'

'Does that matter?'

'It does to me. Martin Fallon, as you call him, is probably the best man I ever knew in my life. A hero.'

'To whom?'

'To the Irish people.'

'Oh, I see. Well, I don't mean him any harm, I can assure you of that.'

'You give me your word on it?'

'Of course.'

'All right, I won't tell you his name, his real name. It doesn't matter anyway. He was a lieutenant in the Provisional IRA. They used to call him the Executioner in Derry. I've never known the likes of him with a gun in his hand. He'd have killed the Pope if he'd thought it would advance the cause. And brains.' He shook his head. 'A university man, Father, would you believe it? Trinity College, no less. There were days when it all poured out of him. Poetry – books. That sort of thing

– and he played the piano like an angel.' O'Hara hesitated, fingering a cirgarette, frowning into the past. 'And then there were other times.'

'What do you mean?' Father da Costa asked him.

'Oh, he used to change completely. Go right inside himself. No emotion, no response. Nothing. Cold and dark.' O'Hara shivered and stuck the cigarette into the corner of his mouth. 'When he was like that, he scared the hell out of everybody, including me, I can tell you.'

'You were with him long?'

'Only for a time. They never really trusted me. I'm a Prod, you see, so I got out.'

'And Fallon?'

'He laid this ambush for a Saracen armoured car, somewhere in Armagh. Mined the road. Someone had got the time wrong. They got a school bus instead with a dozen kids on board. Five killed, the rest crippled. You know how it is. It finished Martin. I think he'd been worrying about the way things were going for a while. All the killing and so on. The business with the bus was the final straw, you might say.'

'I can see that it would be,' Father da Costa said without irony.

'I thought he was dead,' O'Hara said. 'Last I heard, the IRA had an execution squad out after him. Me, I'm no account. Nobody worries about me, but for someone like Martin, it's different. He knows too much. For a man like him, there's only one way out of the movement and that's in a coffin.'

He got to his feet, face flushed. 'Well, Father, I'll be leaving you now. This town and I are parting company.'

He walked to the door and Father da Costa went with him. As rain drifted across the street, O'Hara buttoned up his coat and said cheerfully, 'Have you ever wondered what it's all about, Father? Life, I mean?'

'Constantly,' Father da Costa told him.

'That's honest, anyway. See you in hell, Father.'

He moved off along the pavement, whistling, and Father da Costa went back across the road to the Holy Name. When he went back into the crypt, everything was in good order again. The men had gone and Anna waited patiently on one of the bench seats.

'I'm sorry I had to leave you,' he said, 'but I wanted to speak to the man who knew Fallon. The one who started all the trouble. He went into the pub on the corner.'

'What did you find out?'

He hesitated, then told her. When he was finished, there was pain on her face. She said slowly, 'Then he isn't what he seemed at first.'

'He killed Krasko,' Father da Costa reminded her. 'Murdered him in cold blood. There was nothing romantic about that.'

'You're right, of course.' She groped for her coat and stood up. 'What are you going to do now?'

'What on earth do you expect me to do?' he said half-angrily. 'Save his soul?'

'It's a thought,' she said, slipping her hand into his arm and they went out together.

* * *

There was an old warehouse at the rear of Meehan's premises in Paul's Square and a fire escape gave easy access to its flat roof.

Fallon crouched behind a low wall as he screwed the silencer on to the barrel of the Ceska and peered across through the rain. The two dormer windows at the rear of Meehan's penthouse were no more than twenty yards away and the curtains weren't drawn. He had seen Meehan several times pacing backwards and forwards, a glass in his hand. On one occasion, Rupert had joined him, putting an arm about his neck, but Meehan had shoved him away and angrily from the look of it.

It was a difficult shot at that distance for a handgun, but not impossible. Fallon crouched down, holding the Ceska ready in both hands, aiming at the left-hand window. Meehan appeared briefly and paused, raising a glass to his lips. Fallon fired the silenced pistol once.

In the penthouse, a mirror on the wall shattered and Meehan dropped to the floor. Rupert, who was lying on the couch watching television, turned quickly. His eyes widened.

'My God, look at the window. Somebody took a shot at you.'

Meehan looked up at the bullet hole, the spider's web of cracks, then across at the mirror. He got up slowly.

Rupert joined him. 'You want to know something, ducky? You're getting to be too damn dangerous to know.'

Meehan shoved him away angrily. 'Get me a drink, damn you. I've got to think this thing out.'

A couple of minutes later the phone rang. When he picked up the receiver, he got a call-box signal and then the line cleared as a coin went in at the other end.

'That you, Meehan?' Fallon said. 'You know who this is?'

'You bastard,' Meehan said. 'What are you trying to do?'

'This time I missed because I meant to,' Fallon said. 'Remember that and tell your goons to stay away from Holy Name – and that includes you.'

He put down the receiver and Meehan did the same. He turned, his face white with fury, and Rupert handed him a drink. 'You don't look too good, ducky, bad news?'

'Fallon,' Meehan said between his teeth. 'It was that bastard Fallon and he missed because he wanted to.'

'Never mind, ducky,' Rupert said. 'After all, you've always got me.'

'That's right,' Meehan said. 'So I have. I was forgetting,' and he hit him in the stomach with his clenched fist.

It was late when Fallon got back, much later than he had intended, and there was no sign of Jenny. He took off his shoes and went up the stairs and along the landing to his room quietly.

He undressed, got into bed and lit a cigarette. He was tired. It had certainly been one hell of a day. There was a slight, timid knock on the door. It opened and Jenny came in.

She wore a dark-blue nylon nightdress, her hair was tied back with a ribbon and her face was scrubbed clean. She said, 'Jack Meehan was on the phone about half an hour ago. He says he wants to see you in the morning.'

'Did he say where?'

'No, he just said to tell you it couldn't be more public so you've nothing to worry about. He'll send a car at seven-thirty.'

Fallon frowned. 'A bit early for him, isn't it?'

'I wouldn't know.' She hesitated. 'I waited. You said an hour. You didn't come.'

'I'm sorry,' he said. 'It couldn't be helped, believe me.'

'I did,' she said. 'You were the first man in years who didn't treat me like something you'd scrape off your shoe.'

She started to cry. Wordless, he pulled back the covers and held out a hand. She stumbled across the room and got in beside him.

He switched off the lamp. She lay there, her face against his chest, sobbing, his arms about her. He held her close, stroking her hair with his other hand and after a while, she slept.

10

Exhumation

The car that called to pick Fallon up the following morning at seven-thirty was a black, funeral limousine. Varley was at the wheel dressed in a neat blue serge suit and peaked cap. There was no other passenger.

Fallon climbed into the rear and closed the door. He reached across and slid back the glass window between the driver's compartment and the rest of the car.

'All right,' he said, as Varley moved into gear and drove away. 'Where are we going?'

'The Catholic cemetery.' Fallon, in the act of lighting his first cigarette of the day, started, and Varley said soothingly, 'Nothing to worry about, Mr Fallon. Honest. It's just that

Mr Meehan has an exhumation first thing this morning.'

'An exhumation?' Fallon said.

'That's right. They don't come along very often and Mr Meehan always likes to see to a thing like that personally. He's very particular about his funeral work.'

'I can believe that,' Fallon said. 'What's so special about this case?'

'Nothing really. I suppose he thought you might find it interesting. The man they're digging up is a German. Died about eighteen months ago. His wife couldn't afford to take him back to Germany then, but now she's come into a bit of money, and wants to bury him in Hamburg.' He swung the car out into the main road and added cheerfully, 'It's a fascinating game, the funeral business, Mr Fallon. Always something new happening.'

'I just bet there is,' Fallon said.

They reached the cemetery in ten minutes, and Varley turned in through the gate and drove up the drive, past the chapel and the superintendent's office, following a narrow track.

The grave they were seeking was on top of the hill covered by a canvas awning. At least a dozen people were grouped around it and there was a truck and a couple of cars. Meehan was standing beside one of them talking to a grey-haired man in rubber boots and an oilskin mac. Meehan wore a Homburg hat and his usual melton overcoat and Donner stood beside him holding an umbrella over his head.

As Fallon got out and splashed through the heavy rain towards them, Meehan turned and smiled. 'Ah, there you are. This is Mr Adams, the Public Health Inspector. Mr Fallon is a colleague of mine.'

Adams shook hands and turned back to Meehan. 'I'll see how they're getting on, Mr Meehan.'

He moved away and Fallon said, 'All right, what game are we playing now?'

'No games,' Meehan said. 'This is strictly business and I've a funeral afterwards so I'm busy all morning, but we obviously need to talk. We can do it in the car on the way. For the moment, just stick close to me and pretend to be a member of the firm. This is a privileged occasion. The cemetery superintendent wouldn't be too pleased if he thought an outsider had sneaked in.'

He moved towards the grave, Donner keeping pace with the umbrella, and Fallon followed. The smell was terrible – like nothing he had ever smelt before and when he peered down into the open grave, he saw that it had been sprinkled with lime.

'Two feet of water down there, Mr Meehan,' the Public Health Inspector called. 'No drainage. Too much clay. Means the coffins going to be in a bad state. Probably come to pieces.'

'All in the game,' Meehan said. 'Better have the other one ready.'

He nodded and two of the gravediggers standing by lifted a large oaken coffin out of the back of the truck and put it down near the grave. When they opened it, Fallon saw that it was zinc lined.

The old coffin drops inside and we close

the lid,' Meehan said. 'Nothing to it. The lid has to be welded into place, mind you, in front of the Public Health Inspector, but that's what the law says if you want to fly a corpse from one country to another.'

Just then there was a sudden flurry of movement, and as they turned, the half-dozen men grouped around the grave heaved up the coffin. Webbing bands had been passed underneath, which to a certain extent held things together, but as the coffin came into view, the end broke away and a couple of decayed feet poked through minus their toes.

The smell was even worse now as the half-dozen unfortunate gravediggers lurched towards the new coffin clutching the old. Meehan seemed to enjoy the whole thing hugely and moved in close, barking orders.

'Watch it, now! Watch it! A little bit more to the left. That's it.'

The old coffin dropped into the new, the lid was closed. He turned triumphantly to Fallon. 'I told you there was nothing to it, didn't I? Now let's get moving. I've got a cremation at nine-thirty.'

The gravediggers seemed badly shaken. One of them lit a cigarette, hands trembling, and said to Fallon in a Dublin accent, 'Is it a fact that they're flying him over to Germany this afternoon?'

'So I understand,' Fallon said.

The old man made a wry face. 'Sure and I hope the pilot remembers to wind the windows down.'

Which at least sent Fallon to the car laughing helplessly to himself.

Donner drove and Meehan and Fallon sat in the back seat. Meehan opened a cupboard in the bottom half of the partition between the driver's compartment and the rear and took out a Thermos flask and a half-bottle of Cognac. He half-filled a cup with coffee, topped it up with Cognac and leaned back.

'Last night. That was very silly. Not what I'd call a friendly gesture at all. What did you have to go and do a thing like that for?'

'You said the priest would be left alone,' Fallon told him, 'then sent O'Hara to the crypt to smash it up. Lucky I turned up when I did. As for O'Hara – he and I are old comrades in a manner of speaking. He's cleared off, by the way. You won't be seeing him around here any more.'

'You have been busy.' Meehan poured more Cognac into his coffee. 'I do admit I got just a little bit annoyed with Father da Costa. On the other hand he wasn't very nice when I spoke to him yesterday evening and all I did was offer to help him raise the money to stop that church of his from falling down!'

'And you thought he'd accept?' Fallon laughed out loud. 'You've got to be joking.'

Meehan shrugged. 'I still say that bullet was an unfriendly act.'

'Just like Billy playing Peeping Tom at Jenny Fox's place,' Fallon said. 'When are you going to do something about that worm, anyway! He isn't fit to be out without his keeper.'

Meehan's face darkened. 'He's my brother,' he said. 'He has his faults, but we all have those. Anyone hurts him, they hurt me too.'

Fallon lit a cigarette and Meehan smiled expansively. 'You don't really know me, do you, Fallon? I mean, the other side of me, for instance? The funeral game.'

'You take it seriously.'

It was a statement of fact, not a question and Meehan nodded soberly. 'You've got to have some respect for death. It's a serious business. Too many people are too off-hand about it these days. Now me, I like to see things done right.'

'I can imagine.'

Meehan smiled. 'That's why I thought it might be a good idea to get together like this morning. You could find it very interesting. Who knows, you might even see some future in the business.'

He put a hand on Fallon's knee and Fallon eased away. Meehan wasn't in the least embarrassed. 'Anyway, we'll start you off with a cremation,' he said. 'See what you make of that.'

He poured another coffee, topped it up with more Cognac and leaned back with a contended sigh.

*   *   *

216

The crematorium was called Pine Trees and when the car turned in through the gate, Fallon was surprised to see Meehan's name in gold leaf on the notice-board, one of half-a-dozen directors.

'I have a fifty-one per cent holding in this place,' Meehan said. 'The most modern crematorium in the north of England. You should see the gardens in spring and summer. Costs us a bomb, but it's worth it. People come from all over.'

The superintendent's house and the office were just inside the gate. They drove on and came to a superb, colonnaded building. Meehan tapped on the glass and Donner braked to a halt.

Meehan wound down the window. 'This is what they call a columbarium,' he said. 'Some people like to store the ashes in an urn and keep it on display. There are niches in all the walls, most of them full. We try to discourage it these days.'

'And what would you recommend?' Fallon demanded, irony in his voice.

'Strewing,' Meehan said seriously. 'Scattering

the ashes on the grass and brushing them
in. We come out of the earth, we go back
to it. I'll show you if you like, after the
funeral.'

Fallon couldn't think of a single thing to
say. The man took himself so seriously. It was
really quite incredible. He sat back and waited
for what was to come.

The chapel and the crematorium were in the
centre of the estate and several hundred yards
from the main gate for obvious reasons. There
were several cars parked there already and a
hearse waited with a coffin at the back, Bonati
at the wheel.

Meehan said, 'We usually bring the hearse
on ahead of the rest of the party if the rela-
tions agree. You can't have a cortège
following the coffin these days, not with
present day traffic. The procession gets split
wide open.'

A moment later, a limousine turned out of
the drive followed by three more. Billy was
sitting up front, beside the driver, Meehan

got out of the car and approached, hat in hand, to greet the mourners.

It was quite a performance and Fallon watched, fascinated, as Meehan moved from one group to the next, his face grave, full of concern. He was particularly good with the older ladies.

The coffin was carried into the chapel and the mourners followed it in. Meehan joined on at the end and pulled at Fallon's sleeve. 'You might as well go in. See the lot.'

The service was painfully brief, almost as synthetic as the taped religious music with its heavenly choir background. Fallon was relieved when the proceedings came to an end and some curtains were closed by an automatic device, hiding the coffin from view.

'They pull it through into the funeral room on a movable belt,' Meehan whispered, 'I'll take you round there when they've all moved off.'

He did a further stint with the relatives when they got outside. A pat on the back where it was needed, an old lady's hand held for an instant. It was really quite masterly.

Finally, he managed to edge away and nodded to Fallon. They moved round to the rear of the building, he opened a door and led the way in.

There were four enormous cylindrical furnaces. Two were roaring away, another was silent. The fourth was being raked out by a man in a white coat.

Meehan nodded familiarly. 'Arthur's all we need in here,' he said. 'Everything's fully automatic. Here, I'll show you.'

The coffin Fallon had last seen in the chapel stood waiting on a trolley. 'Rubber doors in the wall,' Meehan explained. 'It comes straight through on the rollers and finishes on the trolley.'

He pushed it across to the cold oven and opened the door. The coffin was at exactly the right height and moved easily on the trolley rollers when he pushed it inside. He closed the door and flicked a red switch. There was an immediate roar and through the glass peep-hole, Fallon could see flames streak into life inside.

'That's all it needs.' Meehan said. 'These

ovens operate by radiant heat and they're the last word in efficiency. An hour from beginning to end and you don't need to worry about pre-heating. The moment it reaches around a thousand degrees centigrade, that coffin will go up like a torch.'

Fallon peered through the glass and saw the coffin suddenly burst into flames. He caught a glimpse of a head, hair flaming, and looked away hurriedly.

Meehan was standing beside the oven where Arthur was busily at work with his rake. 'Have a look at this. This is what you're left with.'

All that remained was a calcined bony skeleton in pieces. As Arthur pushed at it with the rake, it broke into fragments falling through the bars into the large tin box below which already contained a fair amount of ash.

Meehan pulled it out, picked it up and carried it across to a contraption on a bench by the wall. 'This is the pulveriser,' he said, emptying the contents of the tin box into the top. He clamped down the lid. 'Just watch. Two minutes is all it takes.'

221

He flicked a switch and the machine got to work, making a terrible grinding noise. When Meehan was satisfied, he switched off and unscrewed a metal urn on the underside and showed it to Fallon, who saw that it was about three-quarters full of powdery grey ash.

'You notice there's a label already on the urn?' Meehan said. 'That's very important. We do everything in strict rotation. No possibility of a mistake.' He pulled open a drawer in a nearby desk and took out a white card edged in black. 'And the next of kin get one of these with the plot number on. What we call a Rest-in-Peace card. Now come outside and I'll show you the final step.'

It was still raining as they moved along the path at the back of the building between cypress trees. They came out into a lawned area, criss-crossed by box hedges. The edges of the paths were lined with numbered plates.

A gardener was working away beside a wheelbarrow hoeing a flower-bed and Meehan called, 'More work for the undertaker, Fred. Better note it down in your little black book.'

The gardener produced a notebook into which he entered the particulars typed on the urn label. 'Number five hundred and thirty-seven, Mr Meehan,' he said when he'd finished.

'All right, Fred, get it down,' Meehan told him.

The gardener moved to the plate with the correct number and strewed the ashes across the damp grass. Then he got a besom and brushed them in.

Meehan turned to Fallon. 'That's it. The whole story. Ashes to ashes. A Rest-in-Peace card with the right number on it is all that's left.'

They walked back towards the chapel. Meehan said, 'I'd rather be buried myself. It's more fitting, but you've got to give people what they want.'

They went round to the front of the chapel. Billy and Bonati had gone, but Donner was still there and Varley had arrived in the other limousine. The crematorium superintendent appeared, wanting a word with Meehan, and Fallon was for the moment left alone.

The stench of that open grave was still in his nostrils. Just inside the main door to the chapel there was a toilet and he went inside and bathed his face and hands in cold water.

A pane of glass in the small window above the basin was missing and rain drifted through. He stood there for a moment, suddenly depressed. The open grave, the toeless feet protruding from the rotting coffin had been a hell of a start to the day and now this. A man came down to so little in the end. A handful of ashes.

When he went outside, Meehan was waiting for him. 'Well, that's it,' he said. 'Do you want to see another one?'

'Not if I can help it.'

Meehan chuckled. 'I've got two more this morning, but never mind. Varley can take you back to Jenny's place.' He grinned broadly. 'Not worth going out on a day like this unless you have to. I'd stay in if I were you. I mean, it could get interesting. She's a real little firecracker when she gets going is our Jenny.'

'I know,' Fallon said. 'You told me.'

He got into the rear seat of the limousine and Varley drove away. Instead of going down to the main gate, he followed a track that was barely wide enough for the car and round to the right through trees.

'I hope you don't mind, Mr Fallon, but it saves a good mile and a half this way.'

They came to a five-barred gate. He got out, opened it, drove through and got out to close the gate again. The main road was fifty yards farther on at the end of the track.

As they moved down towards the centre of the city, Fallon said, 'You can drop me anywhere here, Charlie.'

'But you can't do that, Mr Fallon. You know you can't,' Varley groaned. 'You know what Mr Meehan said. I've got to take you back to Jenny's place.'

'Well, you tell Mr Meehan, with my compliments, that he can do the other thing.'

They were moving along Rockingham Street now and as they came to the Holy Name, Fallon leaned over suddenly and switched off the ignition. As the car coasted

225

to a halt, he opened the door, jumped out and crossed the road. Varley watched him go into the side entrance of the church, then drove rapidly away to report.

11

The Gospel according to Fallon

The Right Reverend Monsignor Canon O'Halloran, administrator of the pro-cathedral, was standing at his study window when Miller and Fitzgerald were shown in. He turned to greet them, moving towards his desk, leaning heavily on a stick, his left leg dragging.

'Good morning, gentlemen, or is it? Sometimes I think this damned rain is never going to stop.'

He spoke with a Belfast accent and Miller liked him at once and for no better reason than the fact that in spite of his white hair, he looked as if he'd once been a useful heavyweight fighter and his nose had been broken in a couple of places.

Miller said, 'I'm Detective-Superintendent Miller, sir. I believe you know Inspector Fitzgerald.'

'I do indeed. One of our Knights of St Columba stalwarts.' Monsignor O'Halloran eased himself into the chair behind the desk. 'The bishop is in Rome, I'm afraid, so you'll have to make do with me.'

'You got my letter, sir?'

'Oh yes, it was delivered by hand last night.'

'I thought that might save time.' Miller hesitated and said carefully, 'I did ask that Father da Costa should be present.'

'He's waiting in the next room,' Monsignor O'Halloran filled his pipe from an old pouch methodically. 'I thought I'd hear what the prosecution had to say first.'

Miller said, 'You've got my letter. It says it all there.'

'And what do you expect me to do?'

'Make Father da Costa see reason. He must help us in this matter. He must identify this man.'

'If your supposition is correct, the Pope

228

himself couldn't do that, Superintendent,' Monsignor O'Halloran said calmly. 'The secret nature of the confessional is absolute.'

'In a case like this?' Miller said angrily. 'That's ridiculous and you know it.'

Inspector Fitzgerald put a restraining hand on his arm, but Monsignor O'Halloran wasn't in the least put out. He said mildly, 'To a Protestant or a Jew, or indeed to anyone outside the Catholic religion, the whole idea of confession must seem absurd. An anachronism that has no place in this modern world. Wouldn't you agree, Superintendent?'

'When I consider this present situation then I must say I do,' Miller told him.

'The Church has always believed confession to be good for the soul. Sin is a terrible burden and through the medium of confession people are able to relieve themselves of that burden and start again.'

Miller stirred impatiently, but O'Halloran continued in the same calm voice. He was extraordinarily persuasive. 'For a confession to be any good as therapy, it has to be told to someone, which is where the priest comes in.

Only as God's intermediary, of course, and one can only expect people to unburden themselves when they know that what they say is absolutely private and will never be revealed on any account.'

'But this is murder we're talking about, Monsignor,' Miller said. 'Murder and corruption of a kind that would horrify you.'

'I doubt that.' Monsignor O'Halloran laughed shortly and put another match to his pipe. 'It's a strange thing, but in spite of the fact that most people believe priests to be somehow cut off from the real world, I come face to face with more human wickedness in a week than the average man does in a lifetime.'

'Very interesting,' Miller said, 'but I fail to see the relevance.'

'Very well, Superintendent. Try this. During the last war, I was in a German prisoner-of-war camp where escape plans were constantly being frustrated because somebody was keeping the German authorities informed of every move that was made.' He heaved himself up out of his seat and hobbled to the window. 'I knew who it was, knew for months. The man involved told me at confession.'

'And you did nothing?' Miller was genuinely shocked.

'Oh, I tried to reason with him privately, but there was nothing else I could do. No possibility of my even hinting to the others what was going on.' He turned, a weary smile on his face. 'You think it easy carrying that kind of burden, Superintendent? Let me tell you something. I hear confessions at the cathedral regularly. Not a week passes that someone doesn't tell me something for which they could be criminally liable at law.'

Miller stood up. 'So you can't help us then?'

'I didn't say that. I'll talk to him. Hear what he has to say. Would you wait outside for a few minutes?'

'Certainly, but I'd like to see him again in your presence before we leave.'

'As you wish.'

They went out and Monsignor O'Halloran pressed a button on the intercom on his desk. 'I'll see Father da Costa now.'

231

It was a bad business and he felt un-accountably depressed in a personal sense. He stared out at the rainswept garden wondering what on earth he was going to say to da Costa and then the door clicked open behind him.

He turned slowly as da Costa crossed to the desk. 'Michael, what on earth am I going to do with you?'

'I'm sorry, Monsignor,' Father da Costa said formally, 'but this situation was not of my choosing.'

'They never are,' Monsignor O'Halloran said wryly as he sat down. 'Is it true what they suppose? Is this business connected in some way with the confessional?'

'Yes,' Father da Costa said simply.

'I thought so. The Superintendent was right, of course. As he said in his letter, it was the only explanation that made any kind of sense.' He sighed heavily and shook his head. 'I would imagine he intends to take this thing further. Are you prepared for that?'

'Of course,' Father da Costa answered calmly.

232

'Then we'd better get it over with,' Monsignor O'Halloran pressed the button on the intercom again. 'Send in Superintendent Miller and Inspector Fitzgerald.' He chuckled. 'It has a certain black humour, this whole business. You must admit.'

'Has it, Monsignor?'

'But of course. They sent you to Holy Name as a punishment, didn't they? To teach you a little humility and here you are, up to your ears in scandal again.' He smiled wryly, 'I can see the expression on the Bishop's face now.'

The door opened and Miller and Fitzgerald were ushered in again. Miller nodded to da Costa. 'Good morning, Father.'

Monsignor O'Halloran pushed himself up on to his feet again, conscious that somehow the situation demanded it. He said, 'I've discussed this matter with Father da Costa, Superintendent. To be perfectly frank, there doesn't seem to be a great deal I can do.'

'I see, sir.' Miller turned to Father da Costa, 'I'll ask you again, Father, and for the last time. Are you prepared to help us?'

'I'm sorry, Superintendent,' Father da Costa told him.

'So am I, Father.' Miller was chillingly formal now. 'I've discussed the situation with my chief constable and this is what I've decided to do. A report on this whole affair and your part in it goes to the Director of Public Prosecutions today to take what action he thinks fit.'

'And where do you think that will get you?' Monsignor O'Halloran asked him.

'I should think there's an excellent chance that they'll issue a warrant for the arrest of Father da Costa on a charge of being an accessory after the fact of murder.'

Monsignor O'Halloran looked grave and yet he shook his head slowly. 'You're wasting your time, Superintendent. They won't play. They'll never issue such a warrant.'

'We'll see, sir,' Miller turned and went out followed by Fitzgerald.

Monsignor O'Halloran sighed heavily and sat down. 'So there we are. Now we wait.'

'I'm sorry, Monsignor,' Father da Costa said.

'I know, Michael, I know.' O'Halloran looked up at him. 'Is there anything I can do for you? Anything at all?'

'Will you hear my confession, Monsignor?'

'Of course.'

Father da Costa moved round to the side of the desk and knelt down.

When Fallon went into the Church, Anna was playing the organ. It was obviously a practice session. Hymns in the main – nothing complicated. He sat in the front pew listening and after a while she stopped playing abruptly.

He walked up the steps between the choir stalls. 'The curse of the church organist's life, hymns,' he said.

She swung round to face him. 'You're early. Uncle Michael said one o'clock.'

'I'd nothing else to do.'

She stood up. 'Would you like to play?'

'Not at the moment.'

'All right,' she said. 'Then you can take me for a walk. I could do with some air.'

235

Her trenchcoat was in the sacristy. He helped her on with it. It was raining heavily when they went outside, but she didn't seem concerned.

'Where would you like to go?' he asked her.

'Oh, this will do fine. I like churchyards. I find them very restful.'

She took his arm and they followed the path between the old Victorian monuments and gravestones. The searching wind chased leaves amongst the stones so that they seemed like living things crawling along the path in front of them.

They paused beside an old marble mausoleum for Fallon to light a cigarette and it was that precise moment that Billy Meehan and Varley appeared at the side gate. They saw Fallon and the girl at once and ducked back out of sight.

'See, he's still here, 'Varley said. 'Thank God fot that.'

'You go back to Paul's Square and wait for Jack,' Billy said. 'Tell him where I am. I'll keep watch here.'

Varley moved away and Billy slipped in

through the gate and worked his way towards Fallon and Anna, using the monuments for cover.

Anna said, 'I'd like to thank you for what you did last night.'

'It was nothing.'

'One of the men involved was an old friend of yours. O'Hara, wasn't that his name?'

Fallon said quickly, 'No, you've got it wrong.'

'I don't think so,' she insisted. 'Uncle Michael spoke to him after you'd left, in the pub across the road. He told him a great deal about you. Belfast, Londonderry – the IRA.'

'The bastard,' Fallon said bitterly. 'He always had a big mouth, that one. Somebody will be closing his eyes with pennies one of these fine days if he isn't careful.'

'I don't think he meant any harm. Uncle Michael's impression was that he thought a great deal about you.' She hesitated and said carefully, 'Things happen in war sometimes that nobody intends.'

Fallon cut in on her sharply. 'I never go back to anything in thought or deed. It doesn't pay.' They turned into another path and he looked up at the rain. 'God, is it never going to stop? What a world. Even the bloody sky won't stop weeping.'

'You have a bitter view of life, Mr Fallon.'

'I speak as I find and as far as I am concerned, life is one hell of a name for the world as it is.'

'And is there nothing, then?' she demanded. 'Not one single solitary thing worth having in this world of yours?'

'Only you,' he said.

They were close to the presbytery now and Billy Meehan observed them closely with the aid of a pair of binoculars from behind a mausoleum.

Anna stopped walking and turned to face Fallon. 'What did you say?'

'You've no business here.' He made a sweeping gesture with one arm encompassing the whole cemetery. 'This place belongs to the dead and you're still alive.'

'And you?'

There was a long pause and then he said calmly, 'No, it's different for me. I'm a dead man walking. Have been for a long time now.'

She was to remember that remark always as one of the most terrible things she had ever heard in her life.

She stared up at him, those calm, blind eyes fixed on some point in space, and then she reached up and pulled down his head and kissed him hard, her mouth opening in a deliberately provocative gesture.

She pulled way. 'Did you feel that?' she demanded fiercely. 'Did I break through?'

'I think you could say that,' he said in some amazement.

'Good,' she said. 'I'm going in now. I want to change and then I have lunch to get ready. You'd better play the organ or something until my uncle gets back.'

'All right,' Fallon said and turned away.

He had only taken a few steps when she called, 'Oh, and Fallon?' When he turned she was standing in the porch, the door half-open. 'Think of me. Remember me. Concentrate on that. I exist. I'm real.'

She went in and closed the door and Fallon turned and walked away quickly.

It was only when he was out of sight that

Billy moved from the shelter of the mausoleum holding his binoculars in one hand. *Fallon and the priest's nice*. Now that was interesting.

He was about to turn away when a movement at one of the presbytery windows caught his eye. He moved back into cover and raised the binoculars.

Anna was standing at the window and as he watched, she started to unbutton her blouse. His mouth went dry, a hand seemed to squeeze his insides and when she unzipped her skirt and stepped out of it, his hands, clutching the binoculars, started to shake.

The bitch, he thought, and she's Fallon's woman. Fallon's. The ache between his thighs was almost unbearable and he turned and hurried away.

Fallon had been playing the organ for just over an hour when he paused for breath. It had been a long time and his hands were aching, but it was good to get down to it again.

He turned and found Father da Costa

sitting in the front pew watching him, arms folded. 'How long have you been there?' Fallon got up and started down the steps between the choir stalls.

'Half and hour, maybe more,' Father da Costa said. 'You're brilliant, you know that, don't you?'

'Used to be.'

'Before you took up the gun for dear old mother Ireland and that glorious cause?'

Fallon went very still. When he spoke, it was almost in a whisper. 'That's of no interest to you.'

'It's of every interest,' Father da Costa told him. 'To me in particular, for obvious reasons. Good God, man, how could you do what you've done and you with so much music in you?'

'Sir Philip Sidney was reputed to be the most perfect of all knights of the court of Elizabeth Tudor,' Fallon said. 'He composed music and wrote poetry like an angel. In his lighter moments, he and Sir Walter Raleigh herded Irishmen together into convenient spots and butchered them like cattle.'

'All right,' Father da Costa said. 'Point taken. But is that how you see yourself? As a soldier?'

'My father was.' Fallon sat back on the altar rail. 'He was a sergeant in the Parachute Regiment. Killed at Arnhem fighting for the English. There's irony for you.'

'And what happened to you?'

'My grandfather raised me. He had a hill farm in the Sperrins. Sheep mostly – a few horses. I ran happily enough, wild and barefooted, till the age of seven when the new schoolmaster, who was also organist of the church, discovered I had perfect pitch. Life was never the same after that.'

'And you went to Trinity College?'

Fallon frowned slightly. 'Who told you that?'

'Your friend O'Hara. Did you take a degree?'

There was sudden real humour in Fallon's eyes. 'Would you believe me, now, Father, if I told you the farm boy became a doctor of music, no less?'

'Why not?' da Costa replied calmly.

'Beethoven's mother was a cook, but never mind that. The other? How did that start?'

'Time and chance. I went to stay with a cousin of mine in Belfast one weekend in August 1969. He lived in the Falls Road. You may remember what happened.'

Father da Costa nodded gravely. 'I think so.'

'An Orange mob led by B specials swarmed in bent on burning every Catholic house in the area to the ground. They were stopped by a handful of IRA men who took to the streets to defend the area.'

'And you became involved.'

'Somebody gave me a rifle, let's put it that way, and I discovered a strange thing. What I aimed at, I hit.'

'You were a natural shot.'

'Exactly.' Fallon's face was dark and suddenly, he took the Ceska out of his pocket. 'When I hold this, when my finger's on the trigger, a strange thing happens. It becomes an extension, and extension of me personally. Does that make sense?'

'Oh, yes,' Father da Costa said. 'But of

243

the most horrible kind. So you continued to kill.'

'To fight,' Fallon said, his face stony, and he slipped the Ceska back inside his pocket. 'As a soldier of the Irish Republican Army.'

'And it became easier? Each time it became easier.'

Fallon straightened slowly. His eyes were very dark. He made no reply.

Father da Costa said, 'I've just come from a final showdown with Superintendent Miller. Would you be interested to know what he intends?'

'All right, tell me.'

'He's laying the facts before the Director of Public Prosecutions and asking him for a warrant charging me with being an accessory after the fact to murder.'

'He'll never make it stick.'

'And what if he succeeds? Would it cause you the slightest concern?'

'Probably not.'

'Good, honesty at last. There's hope for you yet. And your cause, Fallon. Irish unity or freedom or hatred of the bloody English

244

or whatever it was. Was it worth it? The shooting and bombings. People dead, people crippled?'

Fallon's face was very white now, the eyes jet black, expressionless. 'I enjoyed every golden moment,' he said calmly.

'And the children?' Father da Costa demanded. 'Was it worth that?'

'That was an accident,' Fallon said hoarsely.

'It always is, but at least there was some semblance of reason to it, however mistaken. But Krasko was plain, cold-blooded murder.'

Fallon laughed softly, 'All right, Father, you want answers. I'll try and give you some.' He walked to the altar rail and put a foot on it, leaning an elbow on his knee, chin in hand. 'There's a poem by Ezra Pound I used to like. "Some quick to arm," it says, and then later, "walked eye-deep in hell, believing in old men's lies." Well, that was my cause at the final end of things. Old men's lies. And for that, I personally killed over thirty people assisted at the end of God knows how many more.'

'All right, so you were mistaken. In the

end, violence in that sort of situation gains you nothing. I could have told you that before you started. But Krasko.' Father da Costa shook his head. 'That, I don't understand.'

'Look, we live in different worlds,' Fallon told him. 'People like Meehan – they're renegades. So am L I engage in a combat that's nothing to do with you and the rest of the bloody civilians. We inhabit our own world. Krasko was a whoremaster, a pimp, a drug-pusher.'

'Whom you murdered,' Father da Costa repeated inexorably.

'I fought for my cause, Father,' Fallon said. 'Killed for it, even when I ceased to believe it worth a single-human life. That was murder. But now? Now, I only kill pigs.'

The disgust, the self-loathing were clear in every word he spoke. Father da Costa said with genuine compassion, 'The world can't be innocent with Man in it.'

'And what in the hell is that pearl of wisdom supposed to mean?' Fallon demanded.

'Perhaps I can explain best by telling you a story,' Father da Costa said. 'I spent several years in a Chinese Communist prison camp after being captured in Korea. What they called a special indoctrination centre.'

Fallon could not help but be interested. 'Brainwashing?' he said.

'That's right. From their point of view, I was a special target, the Catholic Church's attitude to Communism being what it is. They have an extraordinarily simple technique and yet it works so often. The original concept is Pavlovian. A question of inducing guilt or rather of magnifying the guilt that is in all of us. Shall I tell you the first thing my instructor asked me? Whether I had a servant at the mission to clean my room and make my bed. When I admitted that I had, he expressed surprise, produced a Bible and read to me that passage in which Our Lord speaks of serving others. Yet here was I allowing one of those I had come to help to serve me. Amazing how guilty that one small point made me feel.'

'And you fell for that?'

'A man can fall for almost anything when he's half-starved and kept in solitary confinement. And they were clever, make no mistake about that. To use the appropriate Marrian terminology, each man has his thesis and his antithesis. For a priest, his thesis is everything he believes in. Everything he and his vocation stand for.'

'And his antithesis?'

'His darker side. The side which is present in all of us. Fear, hate, violence, aggression, the desires of the flesh. This is the side they work on, inducing guilt feelings to such a degree in an attempt to force a complete breakdown. Only after that can they start their own particular brand of re-education.'

'What did they try on you?'

'With me it was sex.' Father da Costa smiled. 'A path they frequently follow where Catholic priests are concerned, celibacy being a state they find quite unintelligible.'

'What did they do?'

'Half-starved me, left me on my own in a damp cell for three months, then put me to bed between two young women who were presumably willing to give their all for the cause, just like you.' He laughed. 'It was

248

rather childish really. The idea was, I suppose, that I should be racked with guilt because I experienced an erection, whereas I took it to be a chemical reaction perfectly understandable in the circumstances. It seemed to me that would be God's view also.'

'So, no sin in you then. Driven snow. Is that it?'

'Not at all. I am a very violent man, Mr Fallon. There was a time in my life when I enjoyed killing. Perhaps if they'd worked on that they would have got somewhere. It was to escape that side of myself that I entered the Church. It was, still is, my greatest weakness, but at least I acknowledged its existence.' He paused and then said deliberately, 'Do you?'

'Any man can know about things,' Fallon said. 'It's knowing the significance of things that's important.'

He paused and Father da Costa said, 'Go on.'

'What do you want me to do, drain the cup?' Fallon demanded. 'The gospel according to Fallon? All right, if that's what you want.'

He mounted the steps leading up to the pulpit and stood at the lectern. 'I never realised you had such a good view. What do you want me to say?'

'Anything you like.'

'All right. We are fundamentally alone. Nothing lasts. There is no purpose to any of it.'

'You are wrong,' Father da Costa said. 'You leave out God.'

'God?' Fallon cried. 'What kind of a God allows a world where children can be happily singing one minute –' here, his voice faltered for a moment – 'and blown into strips of bloody flesh the next. Can you honestly tell me you still believe in a God after what they did to you in Korea? Are you telling me you never faltered, not once?'

'Strength comes from adversity always,' Father da Costa told him. 'I crouched in the darkness in my own filth for six months once, on the end of a chain. There was one day, one moment, when I might have done anything. And then the stone rolled aside and I smelled the grave, saw him walk out on his own two feet and I knew, Fallon I knew!'

'Well, all I can say is, that if he exists, your God, I wish to hell you could get him to make up his mind. He's big on how and when. Not so hot on why.'

'Have you learned nothing, then?' Father da Costa demanded.

'Oh yes,' Fallon said. 'I've learned to kill with a smile, Father, that's very important. But the biggest lesson of all, I learned too late.'

'And what might that be?'

'That nothing is worth dying for.'

It was suddenly very quiet, only the endless rain drifting against the windows. Fallon came down the steps of the pulpit buckling the belt of his trenchcoat. He paused beside Father da Costa.

'And the real trouble is, Father, that nothing's worth living for either.'

He walked away down the aisle, his footsteps echoing. The door banged, the candles flickered. Father da Costa knelt down at the altar rail, folded his hands and prayed as he had seldom prayed before.

After a while, a door clicked open and a

familiar voice said, 'Uncle Michael? Are you there?'

He turned to find Anna standing outside the sacristy door. 'Over here,' he called.

She moved towards him and he went to meet her, reaching for her outstretched hands. He took her across to the front pew and they sat down. And as usual she sensed his mood.

'What is it? she said, her face full of concern, 'Where's Mr Fallon?'

'Gone,' he said. 'We had quite a chat. I think I understand him more now.'

'He's dead inside,' she said. 'Everything frozen.'

'And tacked by self-hate. He hates himself, so he hates all of life. He has no feelings left, not in any normal sense. In fact it is my judgement that the man is probably seeking death. One possible reason for him to continue to lead the life he does.'

'But I don't understand,' she said.

'He puts his whole life on the scales, gave himself for a cause he believed was an honourable one – gave everything he had. A dangerous thing to do, because if anything goes wrong, if you find that in the final analysis your cause is as worthless as a bent farthing, you're left with nothing.'

'He told me he was a dead man walking,' she said.

'I think that's how he sees himself.'

She put a hand on his arm. 'But what can you do?' she said. 'What can anyone do?'

'Help him find himself. Save his soul, perhaps. I don't really know. But I must do something. I must!'

He got up, walked across to the altar rail, knelt down and started to pray.

12

More Work for the Undertaker

Fallon was in the kitchen having tea with Jenny when the doorbell rang. She went to answer it. When she came back, Jack Meehan and Billy followed her into the room.

'All right, sweetheart,' Meehan told her. 'Make yourself scarce. This is business.'

She gave Fallon a brief troubled look, hesitated, then went out. 'She's taken a shine to you, I can see that,' Meehan commented.

He sat on the edge of the table and poured himself a cup of tea. Billy leaned against the wall by the door, hands in his pockets, watching Fallon sullenly.

'She's a nice kid,' Fallon said, 'but you haven't come here to discuss Jenny.'

Meehan sighed. 'You've been a naughty boy again, Fallon. I told you when I left you this morning to come back here and keep under cover and what did you do at the first opportunity? Gave poor old Varley the slip again and that isn't nice because he knows how annoyed I get and he has a weak heart.'

'Make your point.'

'All right. You went to see that bloody priest again.'

'Like hell he did,' Billy put in from the doorway. 'He was with that da Costa bird in the churchyard.'

'The blind girl?' Meehan said.

'That's right. She kissed him.'

Meehan shook his head sorrowfully. 'Leading the poor girl on like that and you leaving the country after tomorrow.'

'She's a right whore,' Billy said viciously. 'Undressing at the bloody window, she was. Anybody could have seen her.'

'That's hardly likely,' Fallon said. 'Not with a twenty-foot wall round the churchyard. I thought I told you to stay away from there.'

'What's wrong?' Billy jeered. 'Frightened I'll queer your pitch? Want to keep it all for yourself?'

Fallon stood up slowly and the look on his face would have frightened the Devil himself. 'Go near that girl again, harm her in any way, and I'll kill you,' he said simply and his voice was the merest whisper.

Jack Meehan turned and slapped his brother across the face backhanded. 'You randy little pig,' he said. 'Sex, that's all you can think about. As if I don't have enough troubles. Go on, get out of it!'

Billy got the door open and glared at Fallon, his face white with passion. 'You wait, you bastard. I'll fix you, you see if I don't. You and your posh bird.'

'I said get out of it!' Meehan roared and Billy did just that, slamming the door behind him.

Meehan turned to Fallon, 'I'll see he doesn't step out of line, don't you worry.'

Fallon put a cigarette between his lips and lit it with a taper from the kitchen fire. 'And you?' he said. 'Who keeps you in line?'

Meehan laughed delightedly. 'Nothing ever throws you, does it? I mean, when Miller walked into church yesterday and found you talking to the priest, I was worried, I can tell you. But when you sat down at that organ.' He shook his head and chuckled. 'That was truly beautiful.'

There was a slight frown on Fallon's face. 'You were there?'

'Oh yes, I was there all right.' Meehan lit a cigarette. 'There's one thing I don't understand.'

'And what would that be?'

'You could have put a bullet in my head last night instead of into that mirror. Why didn't you? I mean, if da Costa is so important to you and you think I'm some sort of threat to him, it would have been the logical thing to do.'

'And what would have happened to my passport and passage on that boat out of Hull Sunday night?'

Meehan chuckled. 'You don't miss a trick, do you? We're a lot alike, Fallon, you and me.'

'I'd rather be the Devil himself,' Fallon told him with deep conviction.

Meehan's face darkened. 'Coming the superior bit again, are we? My life for Ireland. The gallant rebel, gun in hand?' There was anger in his voice now. 'Don't give me that crap, Fallon. You enjoyed it for its own sake, running around in a trenchcoat with a gun in your pocket like something out of an old movie. You enjoyed the killing. Shall I tell you how I know? Because you're too bloody good at it not to have done.'

Fallon sat there staring at him, his face very white, and then, by some mysterious alchemy, the Ceska was in his hand.

Meehan laughed harshly. 'You need me, Fallon, remember? Without me there's no passport and no passage out of Hull Sunday so put it away like a good boy.'

He walked to the door and opened it. Fallon shifted his aim slightly, following him, and Meehan turned to face him. 'All right then, let's see you pull that trigger.'

Fallon held the gun steady. Meehan stood there waiting, hands in the pockets of his overcoat. After a while he turned slowly and went out, closing the door behind him.

For a moment or so longer Fallon held the Ceska out in front of him, staring into space, and then, very slowly, he lowered it, resting his hand on the table, his finger still on the trigger.

He was still sitting there when Jenny came in. 'They've gone,' she said.

Fallon made no reply and she looked down at the gun with distaste. 'What did you need that thing for? What happened?'

'Nothing much,' he said. 'He held up a mirror, that's all, but there was nothing there that I hadn't seen before.' He pushed back his hair and stood up. 'I think I'll get a couple of hours' sleep.'

He moved to the door and she said diffidently. 'Would you like me to come up?'

It was as if he hadn't heard her and went out quietly, trapped in some dark world of his own. She sat down at the table and buried her face in her hands.

*　　*　　*

When Fitzgerald went into Miller's office, the Superintendent was standing by the window reading a carbon copy of a letter.

He offered it to Fitzgerald. 'That's what we sent to the Director of Public Prosecutions.'

Fitzgerald read it quickly. 'That seems to sum up the situation pretty adequately to me, sir,' he said as he handed the letter back. 'When can we expect a decision?'

'That's the trouble, they'll probably take a couple of days. Unofficially, I've already spoken to the man who'll be handling it by telephone.'

'And what did he think, sir?'

'If you really want to know, he wasn't too bloody hopeful.' Miller's frustration was a tanglible thing. 'Anything to do with religion, you know what people are like. That's the English for you.'

'I see, sir,' Fitzgerald said slowly.

It was only then that Miller noticed that the Inspector was holding a flimsy in his right hand. 'What have you got there?'

Fitzgerald steeled himself, 'Bad news, I'm afraid, sir. From CRO about that Ceska.'

Miller sat down wearily. 'All right, tell me the worst.'

'According to the computer, the last time a Ceska was used to kill someone in this country was in June, nineteen fifty-two, sir. A Polish ex-serviceman shot his wife and her lover to death. They hanged him three months later.'

'Marvellous,' Miller said bitterly. 'That's all I needed.'

'Of course they're circulating arms dealers in the London area for us,' Fitzgerald said, 'It will take time, but something could come out of that line of enquiry.'

'I know,' Miller said bitterly. 'Pigs might also fly.' He pulled on his raincoat. 'Do you know what the unique feature of this case is?'

'I don't think so, sir.'

'Then I'll tell you. There's nothing to solve. We already know who's behind the killing. Jack Meehan, and if that damned priest would only open his mouth I could have his head on a platter.'

Miller turned angrily and walked out,

banging the door so hard that the glass panel cracked.

Fallon had only taken off his shoes and jacket and had lain on top of the bed. He awakened to find the room in darkness. He had been covered with an eiderdown which meant that Jenny must have been in. It was just after eight when he checked his watch and he pulled on his shoes hurriedly, grabbed his jacket and went downstairs.

Jenny was doing some ironing when he went into the kitchen. She glanced up. 'I looked in about three hours ago, but you were asleep.'

'You should have wakened me,' he said and took down his raincoat from behind the door.

'Jack Meehan said you weren't to go out.'

'I know.' He transferred the Ceska to the pocket of his raincoat and fastened the belt.

'It's that girl, isn't it?' she said. 'You're worried about her.' He frowned slightly and she rested the iron. 'Oh, I was listening outside the door. I heard most of what went on. What's she like?'

'She's blind,' Fallon said. 'That means she's vulnerable.'

'And you're worried about Billy? You think he might try to pay you off for what happened last night by getting at her?'

'Something like that.'

'I don't blame you.' She started to iron a crisp white blouse. 'Let me tell you about him so you know what you're up against. At twelve, most boys are lucky if they've learnt how to make love to their hand, but not our Billy. At that age, he was having it off with grown women. Whores mostly, working for Jack Meehan, and Billy was Jack's brother, so they didn't like to say no.' She shook her head. 'He never looked back. By the time he was fifteen he was a dirty, sadistic little pervert. It was downhill all the way after that.' She rested the iron again. 'So if I were you, I'd worry all right where he's concerned.'

'Thanks,' he said. 'Don't wait up for me.'

The door banged and he was gone. She

stood there for a moment, staring into space sadly and then she returned to her ironing.

Anna da Costa was about to get into the bath when she heard the phone ringing. She put on a robe and went downstairs, arriving in the hall as her uncle replaced the receiver.

'What is it?' she asked.

'The Infirmary. The old Italian lady I visited the other day. She's had a relapse. They expect her to die some time tonight. I'll have to go.'

She took down his coat from the hallstand and held it out for him. He opened the front door and they moved out into the porch. The rain was pouring down.

'I'll walk,' he said. 'It's not worth taking the van. Will you be all right?'

'Don't worry about me,' she said. 'How long will you be?'

'God knows, probably several hours. Don't wait up for me.'

He plunged into the rain and hurried down the path passing a magnificent Victorian mausoleum, the pride of the cemetery with its bronze doors and marble porch. Billy Meehan dropped back into the shadows of the porch quickly, but when the priest had gone past, he moved forward again.

He had heard the exchange at the door and a cold finger of excitement moved in his belly. He had already had intercourse twice that night with a prostitute, not that it had been any good. He didn't seem to be able to get any satisfaction any more. He'd intended going home and then he'd remembered Anna – Anna at the window undressing.

He'd only been lurking in the shadows of that porch for ten minutes, but he was already bitterly cold and rain drifted in on the wind. He thought of Fallon, the humiliation of the previous night, and his face contorted.

'The bastard,' he said softly. 'The little Mick bastard. I'll show him.'

He produced a half-bottle of Scotch from his pocket and took a long pull.

Father da Costa hurried into the church. He took a Host out of the ciborium and hung it in a silver pyx around his neck. He also took holy oils with him to anoint the dying woman's ears, nose, mouth, hands and feet and went out quietly.

The church was still and quiet, only the images floating in candlelight, the drift of rain against the window. It was perhaps five minutes after Father da Costa's departure that the door creaked open eerily and Fallon entered.

He looked about him to make sure that no one was there, then hurried down the aisle, went inside the cage and pressed the button to ascend. He didn't go right up to the tower, stopping the cage on the other side of the canvas sheet covering the hole in the roof of the nave.

It only sloped slightly and he walked across the sheeting lead and paused at the low retaining wall, sheltering in the angle of a buttress with the tower.

From here, his view of the presbytery was excellent and two tall concrete lamp-posts in the street to the left towered above the cemetery walls, throwing a band of light across the front of the house.

There was a light in one of the bedroom windows and he could see right inside the room. A wardrobe, a painting on the wall, the end of a bed and then Anna suddenly appeared wrapped in a large white towel.

From the look of things she had obviously just got out of the bath. She didn't bother to draw the curtains, probably secure in the knowledge that she was cut off from the street by twenty-foot high walls or perhaps it was something to do with her blindness.

As Fallon watched she started to dry herself off. Strange how few women looked at their best in the altogether, he told himself, but she was more than passable. The black hair almost reached the pointed breasts and a narrow waist swelled to hips that were perhaps a trifle too large for some tastes.

She pulled on a pair of hold-up stockings, black bra and pants and a green, silk dress with a pleated skirt and started to brush her hair, perhaps the most womanly of all actions. Fallon felt strangely sad, no desire in him at all, certainly not for anything physical.

267

Just the sudden terrible knowledge that he was looking at something he could never have on top of this earth and there was no one to blame but himself. She tied her hair back with a black ribbon and moved out of sight. A second later, the light went off.

Fallon shivered as the wind drove rain in his face and turned up his collar. It was very quiet, only the occasional sound of a car muted in the distance, and then, quite clearly, he heard the crunch of a foot in the gravel on the path below.

As he peered down, a figure moved out of the shadows into the light, the white shoulder-length hair identifying him at once. *Billy Meehan*. As Fallon leaned forward, the boy mounted the steps to the front door and tried the handle. It opened to his touch and he passed inside.

Fallon turned and scrambled back across the roof to the hoist. He jumped inside the cage, closed the gate and pressed the button to descend, his heart racing.

*　　*　　*

The sight of Anna at the window had excited Billy Meehan to a state where he could no longer contain himself. The ache between his legs was unbearable and the half-bottle of whisky which he had consumed had destroyed completely any last vestige of self-control.

He moved into the porch and tried the door and when it opened to his touch, he almost choked with excitement. He tiptoed inside, closing it behind him, and pushed the bolt home.

He could hear someone singing softly from a room at the end of the passage. He approached quietly and peered in through the partly opened door.

Anna was sitting at one end of a Victorian sofa, a small table at her elbow and the large sewing-box which stood on it was open, She was sewing a button on a shirt and as he watched, she reached into the mending-box, fumbled for a pair of scissors and cut the thread.

Billy took off his overcoat, dropped it to the floor and moved towards her, shaking with excitement. She was aware first of the coat dropping and then the faint sound of his approach and frowned, her face turned towards him.

'Who is it? Is anyone there?'

He paused momentarily and she stood up. Billy approached on tiptoe and as she half-turned, clutching the shirt to her, a needle in the other hand, he circled behind her.

'Who is it?' she demanded, fear in her voice.

He slipped a hand up her skirt from the rear, cupping it between her thighs and giggled. 'That's nice. You like that, don't you? Most girls like what I do to them.'

She gave a cry of horror, pulling away, turning to face him at the same moment and he reached forward and slipped a hand inside the neck of her dress feeling for a breast.

Anna cried out, her face a mask of horror. 'No, please – in the name of God! Who is it?'

'Fallon!' he said. 'It's me, Fallon!'

'Liar!' she screamed. 'Liar!' and lashed out blindly, catching him across the face.

Billy slapped her back-handed. 'I'll teach you, you bitch. I'll make you crawl.'

He knocked her back across the sofa tearing at her pants, forcing her thighs apart brutally, crushing his mouth on hers. Through the unbelievable horror of it, the nameless disgust, she was aware of his hand between his legs fumbling with the zip of his trousers and then the hardness pushing against her.

She screamed, he slapped her again, forcing her head back across the end of the sofa and her right hand, grabbing at the table for support, fastened upon the scissors. She was almost unconscious by then so that as the darkness flooded over her, she was not aware of her hand swinging convulsively, driving the scissors up under the ribs with all the force of which she was capable, piercing the heart and killing him instantly.

Finding the front door barred. Fallon had only been able to gain entry by breaking a kitchen window. He arrived in the sitting-room to find Billy Meehan sprawled across the unconscious girl and hurled himself on him. It was only in dragging him away that he saw the handle of the scissors protruding beneath the ribs.

He picked her up in his arms and carried her upstairs. The first room he tried was obviously her uncle's, but the second was hers and he laid her on the bed and covered her with an eiderdown.

He sat there holding her hand and after a while her eyelids flickered. She started violently and tried to pull her hands away.

Fallon said soothingly, 'There, now, it's me – Martin Fallon. You're all right now. You've nothing to worry about.'

She gave a great shuddering sigh. 'Thank God! Thank God! What happened?'

'Can't you remember?'

'Only this dreadful man. He said he was you and then he tried to . . . he tried to . . .' She shuddered. 'Oh, God, the feel of his hands. It was horrible. Horrible. I fainted, I think.'

'That's right,' Fallon said calmly. 'Then I arrived and he ran away.'

She turned her face to him, those blind eyes focusing to one side. 'Did you see who it was?'

'I'm afraid not.'

'Was it . . .' She hesitated. 'Do you think Meehan was behind it?'

'I should imagine so.'

She closed her eyes and when Fallon gently took her hand, she pulled it away convulsively. It was as if for the moment she could not bear the touch of a man – any man.

He steeled himself for the obvious question. 'Did he have his way with you?'

'No, I don't think so.'

'Would you like me to get you a doctor?'

'For God's sake, no, not that. The very idea that anyone should know fills me with horror.'

'And your uncle?'

'He's attending a dying woman at the infirmary. He could be hours.'

Fallon stood up. 'All right – stay here and rest. I'll bring you a brandy.'

She closed her eyes again. The lids were pale, translucent. She seemed very vulnerable and Fallon went down the stairs full of controlled, ice-cold anger.

He dropped to one knee beside Billy Meehan, took out a handkerchief, wrapped it around the handle of the scissors and pulled them out. There was very little blood and obviously most of the bleeding was internal.

He cleaned the scissors, then went to the door and picked up the boy's overcoat. Some car keys fell to the floor. He picked them up mechanically, then draped the coat across the body.

As he looked down at it, he was conscious only of disgust and loathing. The world was well rid of Billy Meehan. His ending had been richly deserved, but could Anna da Costa live with the knowledge that she had killed him? And even if the verdict of the court was as it should be – even if she were exonerated, the whole world would know. At the thought of the shame, the humiliation for that gentle creature, Fallon's anger was so great that he kicked the corpse in the side.

And in the same moment, a thought came to him that was so incredible it almost took his breath away. What if she didn't have to know, now or ever? What if Billy Meehan vanished utterly and completely from the face of the earth as if he had never existed? There was a way. It could be done. In any event, he owed it to her to try.

The keys which had fallen from the overcoat pocket indicated the presence of Billy's car somewhere in the vicinity and if it was the red Scimitar, it should be easy enough to find. Fallon let himself out of the front door, hurried through the cemetery to the side gate.

The Scimitar was parked at the kerb only a few yards away. He unlocked the tailgate and when he opened it, Tommy, the grey whippet, barked once, then nuzzled his hand. The presence of the dog was unfortunate, but couldn't be helped. Fallon closed the tailgate and hurried back to the presbytery.

He pulled off the overcoat and went through the boy's pockets systematically, emptying them of everything they held. He removed a gold medallion on a chain around the neck, a signet ring and a wrist-watch and put them in his pocket, then he wrapped the body in the overcoat, heaved it over his shoulder and went out.

He paused at the gate to make sure that the coast was clear, but the street was silent and deserted. He crossed to the Scimitar quickly, heaved up the tailgate with one hand and dumped the body inside. The whippet started to whine almost immediately and he closed the tailgate quickly and went back to the presbytery.

He washed the scissors thoroughly in hot water in the kitchen, went back to the sitting-room and replaced them in the mending-box. Then he poured a little brandy in a glass and took it upstairs.

She was already half asleep, but sat up to drink the brandy. Fallon said, 'What about your uncle? Do you want him to know what happened?'

'Yes – yes, I think so. It's right that he should know.'

'All right,' Fallon said, and he tucked the quilt around her. 'Go to sleep now. I'll be downstairs. You've nothing to worry about. I'll wait till your uncle comes back.'

'He might be hours,' she said sleepily.

'That's all right.'

He walked to the door, 'I'm sorry to be such a nuisance,' she whispered.

'I brought you to this,' he said. 'If it hadn't been for me none of this would have happened.'

'It's pointless to talk like that,' she said. 'There's a purpose to everything under heaven – a reason – even for my blindness. We can't always see it because we're such little people, but it's there.'

He was strangely comforted by her words, God knows why, and said softly, 'Go to sleep now,' and closed the door.

Time, now, was the critical factor and he quietly let himself out of the front door and hurried through the churchyard to the Scimitar.

Strangely enough, the whippet gave him no trouble during the drive. It crouched in the rear beside the body, whining only occasionally, although when he put a hand on it, it was trembling.

He approached Pine Trees Crematorium

by the back lane Varley had used that
morning, getting out of the car to open the
five-barred gate that led into the estate. He
followed the same narrow track down
through the cypress trees, cutting the engine
for the last hundred yards which was slightly
downhill. Not that it mattered, for as he
remembered it, the superintendent's house
and the main gate were a good quarter of a
mile from the crematorium itself, so noise
was really no problem.

He left the Scimitar at the side of the chapel
and gained access by reaching in through the
broken pane in the lavatory which he had
noticed during his visit that morning and
unfastening the window itself.

The chapel door had a Yale lock so it
opened easily enough from the inside. He
returned to the Scimitar. There was a torch
in the glove compartment which he slipped
into his pocket, then he raised the tailgate
and heaved the body over his shoulder. The
whippet tried to follow, but he managed to
shove it back inside with his free hand and
closed the tailgate again.

He gained access to the furnace room by sliding the body along the rollers of the movable belt and crawling through after it himself, following the route the coffin had taken that morning.

The furnaces were cold and dark. He opened the door of the first one and shoved the body inside. Next he produced the various items he had taken from Billy Meehan's pockets and examined them in the light of the torch. Those things which would burn, he placed on top of the body. The ring, the watch and the medal he put back in his pocket. Then he closed the oven door and pressed the switch.

He could hear the muted rumble of the gas jets as they roared into life and peered inside. What was it Meehan had said? An hour at the most. He lit a cigarette, opened the back door and went outside.

The sound of the furnace in operation was barely discernible outside the building. Not at all when he moved a few yards away. He went back inside to see what was happening. The gauge was just coming up to the thousand degrees centigrade mark and as he peered through the observation panel in the door, the wallet he had left on the body's chest burst into flames. The clothing was already smouldering, there was a sudden bright flash and the whole body started to burn.

He lit another cigarette, went and stood at the back door and waited.

At the end of the specified period he switched off. There was part of the skull, the pelvic girdle and some of the limbs clearly visible, and much of this crumbled into even smaller pieces at the first touch of the rake.

He filled the tin box, found a handbrush and shovel, carefully swept up every trace of ash that he could see, then closed the furnace door leaving it exactly as he had found it. Certainly all heat would be dissipated again before the morning.

He found an empty urn, screwed it on the bottom of the pulveriser then poured in the contents of the tin box. He clamped down the lid and switched on. While he was waiting, he opened the desk drawer and helped himself to a blank Rest-in-Peace card.

When he switched off about two minutes later and unscrewed the urn, all that was left of Billy Meehan was about five pounds of grey ash.

He walked along the path to the point Meehan had taken him to that morning until he came across a gardener's wheelbarrow and various tools, indicating where the man had stopped work that afternoon.

Fallon checked the number plate and strewed the ashes carefully. Then he took a besom from the wheelbarrow and worked them well in. When he was satisfied, he replaced the besom exactly as he had found it, turned and walked away.

It was when he reached the Scimitar that he ran into his first snag for as he opened the door to get behind the wheel, the whippet slipped through his legs and scampered away.

Fallon went after it fast. It went round the corner of the chapel and followed the path he had just used. When he reached the place where he had strewn the ashes, the whippet was crouching in the wet grass, whining very softly.

Fallon picked him up and fondled his ears, talking softly to his as he walked back. When he got behind the wheel this time, he held on to the animal until he had closed the door. He put it in the rear seat and drove away quickly.

It was only after he had closed the five-barred gate behind him and turned into the main road again that he allowed that iron composure of his to give a little. He gave a long shuddering sigh, a partial release of tension, and when he lit a cigarette his hands were trembling.

It had worked and there was a kind of elation in that. For a while it had seemed that Billy Meehan might prove to be just as malignant an influence in death as he had been in life, but not now. He had ceased to exist, had been wiped clean off the face of the earth, and Fallon felt not even a twinge of compunction.

As far as he was concerned, Billy Meehan had been from under a stone, not fit to wipe Anna da Costa's shoes. Let be.

When he reached Paul's Square, he turned into the mews entrance cautiously, but luck was with him to the very end. The yard was deserted. He ran the Scimitar into the garage, left both the keys and the whippet inside and walked rapidly away.

When he got back to the presbytery, there was no sign of Father da Costa. Fallon went upstairs on tiptoe and peered into Anna's bedroom. She was sleeping soundly so he closed her door and went back downstairs.

He went into the sitting-room and checked the carpet carefully, but there was no sign of blood. So that was very much that. He went to the sideboard and poured himself a large whisky. As he was adding a dash of soda, the front door opened.

Fallon turned round as Father da Costa entered the room. The priest stopped short in amazement. 'Fallon, what are you doing here?' And then he turned very pale and said, 'Oh, dear God! Anna!'

He turned and moved to the stairs and Fallon went after him. 'She's all right. She's sleeping.'

Father da Costa turned slowly. 'What happened?'

'There was an intruder,' Fallon said. 'I arrived in time to chase him away.'

'One of Meehan's men?'

Fallon shrugged. 'Maybe – I didn't get a good look at him.'

Father da Costa paced up and down the hall, fingers intertwined so tightly that the knuckles turned white. 'Oh, my God! he said. When will it all end?'

'I'm leaving on Sunday night,' Fallon told him. 'They've arranged passage for me on a ship out of Hull.'

'And you think that will finish it?' Father da Costa shook his head. 'You're a fool, Fallon.

Jack Meehan will never feel safe while I am still in the land of the living. Trust, honour, truth, the sanctity of the given word. None of these exist for him personally so why should he believe that they have a meaning for someone else?'

'All right,' Fallon said. 'It's all my fault. What do you want me to do?'

'There's only one thing you can do,' Father da Costa said. 'Set me free in the only way possible.'

'And spend my life in a maximum security cell?' Fallon shook his head. 'I'm not that kind of hero.'

He walked to the front door and Father da Costa said, 'She *is* all right?'

Fallon nodded soberly. 'A good night's rest is all she needs. She's a much stronger person than you realise. In every way.'

He turned to go out and Father da Costa said, 'That you arrived when you did was most fortuitous.'

'All right,' Fallon said. 'So I was watching the house.'

Father da Costa shook his head sadly. 'You see, my friend, good deeds in spite of yourself. You are a lost man.'

'Go to hell!' Fallon said and he plunged out into the rain and walked rapidly away.

13

The Church Militant

Father da Costa was packing his vestment into
a small suitcase when Anna went into the study.
It was a grey morning, that eternal rain still
tapping at the window. She was a little paler
than usual, but otherwise seemed quite
composed. Her hair was tied back with a black
ribbon and she wore a neat grey skirt and
sweater.

Father da Costa took both her hands and
led her to the fire. 'Are you all right?'

'I'm fine,' she said. 'Truly I am. Are you
going out?'

'I'm afraid I have to. One of the nuns at
the convent school of Our Lady of Pity died
yesterday. Sister Marie Gabrielle. They've

asked me to officiate.' He hesitated. 'I don't like leaving you.'

'Nonsense,' she said. 'I'll be all right. Sister Claire will be bringing up the children from the junior school for choir practice at ten-thirty. I have a private lesson after that until twelve.'

'Fine,' he said. 'I'll be back by then.'

He picked up his case and she took his arm and they went through to the hall together. 'You'll need your raincoat.'

He shook his head. 'The umbrella will be enough.' He opened the door and hesitated, 'I've been thinking, Anna. Perhaps you should go away for a while. Just until this thing is settled one way or the other.'

'No!' she said firmly.

He put down his case and took her by the shoulders standing there in the half-open doorway. 'I've never felt so helpless. So confused. After what happened last night, I thought of speaking to Miller.'

'But you can't do that,' she said quickly – too quickly. 'Not without involving Fallon.'

He gazed at her searchingly, 'You like him, don't you?'

'It's not the word I would choose,' she said calmly. 'I feel for him. He has been marked by life. No, used by life in an unfair way. Spoiled utterly.' There was a sudden passion in her voice. 'No one could have the music in him that man has and have no soul. God could not be so inhuman.'

The greatest gift God gave to man was free will, my dear. Good and evil. Each man has a free choice in the matter.'

'All right,' she said fiercely. 'I only know one thing with any certainty. When I needed help last night, more than I have ever needed it in my life before, it was Fallon who saved me.'

'I know,' Father da Costa told her. 'He was watching the house.'

Her entire expression changed, colour touched those pale cheeks. 'And you don't care what happens to him?'

'Oh, I care,' Father da Costa said gravely. 'More than you perhaps understand. I see a man of genius brought down to the level of the gutter. I see a human being – a fine human being – committing, for his own dark reasons, a kind of personal suicide.'

'Then help him.' she said.

'To help himself?' Father da Costa shook his head sadly. 'That only works in books. Seldom in life. Whoever he is, this man who calls himself Martin Fallon, one thing is certain. He hates himself for what he has done, for what he has become. He is devoured by self-loathing.'

But by now she looked completely bewildered. 'I don't understand this – not any of it.'

'He is a man who seeks Death at every turn, Anna. Who would welcome him with open arms.' He shook his head. 'Oh yes, I care what happens to Martin Fallon – care passionately. The tragedy is that he does not.'

He turned and left her there in the porch and hurried away through the churchyard, head down against the rain, not bothering to raise his umbrella. When he moved into the side porch to unlock the sacristy door, Fallon was sitting on the small bench leaning against the corner, head on his chest, hands in the pockets of his trenchcoat.

Father da Costa shook him by the shoulder

and Fallon raised his head and opened his eyes instantly. He badly needed a shave and the skin of his face seemed to have tightened over the cheekbones and the eyes were vacant.

'A long night,' Father da Costa said gently.

'Time to think,' Fallon said in a strange, dead voice. 'About a lot of things.'

'Any conclusions?'

'Oh yes.' Fallon stood up and moved out into the rain. 'The right place for me, a cemetery.' He turned to face da Costa, a slight smile on his lips. 'You see, Father, I've finally realised one very important thing.'

'And what's that?' Father da Costa asked him.

'That I can't live with myself any more.'

He turned and walked away very quickly and Father da Costa moved out into the rain, one hand extended as if he would pull him back.

'Fallon,' he called hoarsely.

A few rooks lifted out of the tree on the other side of the churchyard, fluttering in the wind like a handful of dirty black rags, calling angrily. As they settled again, Fallon turned the corner of the church and was gone.

When Anna closed the front door of the presbytery and went down the steps, she was instantly aware of the organ. She stood quite still, looking across the cemetery towards the church, head slightly turned as she listened. The playing, of course, was quite unmistakable. The heart quickened inside her, she hurried along the path as fast as she dared, tip-tapping with her stick.

When she opened the sacristy door, the music seemed to fill the church. He was playing Pavane for a Dead Infanta, infinitely moving, touching the very heart of things, the deep places of life, brilliant technique and emotion combining in a way she would never have thought possible.

He finished on a dying fall and sat, shoulders hunched for a long moment as the last echoes died away. When he swung round on the stool, she was standing at the altar rail.

'I've never heard such playing,' she told him.

He went down through the choir stalls and stood on the other side of the rail from her. 'Good funeral music.'

His words touched the heart of her like a cold finger. 'You mustn't speak like that.' She forced a smile. 'Did you want to see me?'

'Let's say I hoped you'd come.'

'Here I am, then.'

'I want you to give your uncle a message. Tell him I'm sorry, more sorry than I can say, but I intend to put things right. You'll have nothing more to worry about, either of you. He has my word on that.'

'But how?' she said. 'I don't understand.'

'My affair,' Fallon told her calmly. 'I started it, I'll finish it. Goodbye, Anna da Costa. You won't see me again.'

'I never have,' she said sadly, and put a hand on his arm as he went by. 'Isn't that a terrible thing?'

He backed away slowly and delicately, making not the slightest sound. Her face changed. She put out a hand uncertainly. 'Mr Fallon?' she said softly. 'Are you there?'

Fallon moved quickly towards the door. It creaked when he opened it and as he turned to look at her for the last time, she called, 'Martin, come back!' and there was a terrible desperation in her voice.

Fallon went out, the door closed with a sigh and Anna da Costa, tears streaming down her face, fell on her knees at the altar rail.

The Little Sisters of Pity were not only teachers. They also had an excellent record in medical missionary work overseas, which was where Father da Costa had first met Sister Marie Gabrielle in Korea in nineteen fifty-one. A fierce little French-woman who was probably the kindest, most loving person he had met in his entire life. Four years in a communist prison camp had ruined her health, but that indomitable spirit, that all-embracing love, had not been touched in the slightest.

Some of the nuns, being human, were crying as they sang the offertory; *'Domine*

Jesu Christ, Rex Glorias, libera animas omnium fidelium . . .'

Their voices rose sweetly to the rafters of the tiny convent chapel as Father da Costa prayed for the repose of Sister Marie Gabrielle's soul, for all sinners everywhere whose actions only cut them off from the infinite blessing of God's love. For Anna, that she might come to no harm. For Martin Fallon that he might face what must be done and for Dandy Jack Meehan . . .

But here, a terrible thing happened, for his throat went dry and he seemed to choke on the very name.

Once the Mass was over and the absolutions given, the nuns carried the coffin out through the rain to the small private cemetery in a corner between the inner and outer walls of the convent.

At the graveside Father da Costa sprinkled the grave and the coffin with holy water and incensed them and after he had prayed, some of the nuns lit candles, with some difficulty because of the rain, to symbolise Sister Marie Gabrielle's soul, with God now and shining still, and they sang together, very sweetly, the twenty-third psalm which had been her favourite.

Father da Costa remembered her, for a moment, during those last days, the broken body racked with pain. Oh God, he thought, why is it the good who suffer? People like Sister Marie Gabrielle?

And then there was Anna. So gentle, so loving, and at the thought of what had taken place the night before, black rage filled his heart.

Try as he might, the only thought that would come to mind as he looked down into the open grave was that Meehan's firm had probably made the coffin.

Jenny Fox had taken two sleeping pills the previous night and overslept. It was after eleven when she awakened and she put on her dressing-gown and went downstairs. She went into the kitchen and found Fallon sitting at the table, the bottle of Irish whiskey in front of him, a half-filled tumbler at his elbow.

He had taken the Ceska to pieces and was putting it carefully together again. The silencer was also on the table next to the whiskey bottle.

'You're starting early,' she commented.

'A long time since I had a drink,' he said. 'A real drink, Now I've had four. I had some thinking to do.'

He emptied his glass in a single swallow, rammed the magazine into the butt of the Ceska and screwed the silencer on the end of the barrel.

Jenny said wearily, 'Did you come to any conclusions?'

'Oh yes, I think you could say that.' He poured himself another whiskey and tossed it down. 'I've decided to start a Jack Meehan-must-go campaign. A sort of one man crusade, if you like.'

'You must be crazy,' she said. 'You wouldn't stand a chance.'

'He'll be sending for me some time today, Jenny. He has to because he's shipping me out from Hull tomorrow night so we've got things to discuss.'

He squinted along the barrel of the gun and Jenny whispered, 'What are you going to do?'

'I'm going to kill the bastard,' he said simply. 'You know what Shakespeare said. A good deed in a naughty world.'

He was drunk, she realised that, but in his own peculiar way. She said desperately. 'Don't be a fool. Kill him and there'll be no passage out of Hull for you. What happens then?'

'I couldn't really care less.'

He flung up his arm and fired. There was a dull thud and a small china dog on the top shelf above the refrigerator shattered into fragments.

'Well now,' he said. 'If I can hit that at this range after half-a bottle of whiskey, I don't see how I can very well miss Dandy Jack.'

He stood up and picked up the bottle of whiskey. Jenny said, 'Martin, listen to me for God's sake.'

He walked past her to the door. 'I didn't go to bed last night so I will now. Wake me if Meehan calls, but whatever happens, don't

298

let me sleep past five o'clock. I've got things to do.'

He went out and she stood there listening as he mounted the stairs. She heard the door of his bedroom open and close and only then did she move, going down on her hands and knees wearily to pick up the shattered fragments of the china dog.

The Bull and Bell yard was not far from Paul's Square, a dirty and sunless cobbled alley named after the public house which had stood there for two hundred years or more. Beside the entrance to the snug stood several overflowing dustbins and cardboard boxes and packing cases were thrown together in an untidy heap.

The Bull and Bell itself did most of its trade in the evening, which was why Jack Meehan preferred to patronise it in the afternoon. For one thing it meant that he could have the snug to himself, which was handy for business of a certain kind.

He sat on a stool, a tankard of beer at his

elbow, finishing a roast beef sandwich and reading the *Financial Times*. Donner was sitting in the window seat playing solitaire.

Meehan emptied his tankard and pushed it across the bar. 'Same again, Harry.'

Harry was a large, hefty young man who, in spite of his white apron, had the physique of a professional Rugby player. He had long dark sideburns and a cold, rather dangerous-looking face.

As he filled the tankard and pushed it across, the door opened and Rupert and Bonati came in. Rupert was wearing a sort of caped, ankle-length highwayman's coat in large checks.

He shook himself vigorously and unbuttoned his coat. 'When's it going to stop, that's what I'd like to know.'

Meehan drank some more beer and belched. He said, 'What in the hell do you want? Who's minding the shop?'

Rupert slid gracefully on to the stool next to him and put a hand on his thigh. 'I do have to eat some time, ducky. I mean, I need to keep my strength up, don't I?'

'All right, Harry.' Meehan said, 'Give him his Bloody Mary.'

Rupert said, 'By the way, does anyone know where Billy is?'

'I haven't seen him since last night,' Meehan told him. 'Who wants him, anyway?'

'The superintendent of Pine Trees phoned into the office just before I left.'

'And what did he want?'

'It seems they found Billy's whippet wandering about up there. Soaked to the skin and trembling life a leaf apparently. Wanted to know what to do with him.'

Meehan frowned. 'What in the hell would it be doing up there?'

Donner said, 'Last I saw of it, was about half eight this morning when I went into the garage. It was inside the Scimitar. I figured Billy had forgotten about it when he came in last night so I let it out. I mean, he's done that before when he's been pissed or something. Left Tommy in the car, I mean.'

'He still hadn't come in when I came out this morning,' Meehan said, 'and if he left his car in the garage, that means he went to one of the city centre clubs. Probably still in bed with some whore, the dirty little bastard.' He turned to Bonati. 'You'd better go up to Pine Trees and get it. Take it back home and give it something to eat.'

'All right, Mr Meehan,' Bonati said and went out.

Meehan swallowed some more beer. 'Inconsiderate little swine. I'll kick his arse for him when I see him.'

'He's young, Mr Meehan,' Harry said. 'He'll learn.'

He picked up a bucket of slops, moved from behind the bar, and opened the door and went out into the yard. As he emptied the bucket across the cobbles, Father da Costa entered the yard. He was wearing his cassock and held the umbrella over his head against the rain.

Harry looked him over in some amazement and Father da Costa said politely, 'I'm looking for Mr Meehan – Mr Jack Meehan. They told me at his office that I might find him here.'

'Inside,' Harry said.

He moved into the snug and Father da Costa followed, pausing just inside the door to put down his umbrella.

It was Rupert who saw him first in the mirror behind the bar. 'Good God Almighty!' he said.

There was a long silence and Meehan turned on his stool very slowly. 'And what in the hell are you doing there? Rattling the box for Christmas or something? Will a quid get rid of you?'

He took out his wallet ostentatiously and Father da Costa said quietly, 'I was hoping we might have a few words in private.'

He stood there with the umbrella in his hand, the skirts of his cassock soaking wet from the long grass of the convent cemetery, mud on his shoes, grey beard tangled, waiting for some sort of response.

Meehan laughed out loud. 'God, but I wish you could see yourself. You look bloody ridiculous. Men in skirts.' He shook his head. 'It'll never catch on.'

Father da Costa said patiently, 'I don't expect it will. Now can we talk?'

Meehan indicated Donner and Rupert with a wave of the hand. 'There's nothing you can say to me that these two can't hear.'

'Very well,' Father da Costa said. 'It's simple enough. I want you to stay away from Holy Name and I don't want any repetition of what happened at the presbytery last night.'

Meehan frowned, 'What in the hell are you talking about?'

'All right, Mr Meehan,' Father da Costa said wearily. 'Last night, someone broke into the presbytery when I was out and attacked my niece. If Fallon hadn't arrived at the right moment and chased the man away anything might have happened to her. On the other hand, I suppose you'll now tell me that you know nothing about it.'

'No, I bloody well don't.' Meehan shouted.

Father da Costa struggled to contain his anger. 'You're lying,' he said simply.

Meehan's face was suffused with blood, the eyes bulging. 'Who in the hell do you think you are?' he demanded hoarsely.

'It's my final warning,' Father da Costa said. 'When we last spoke I told you my God was a God of Wrath as well as of Love. You'd do well to remember that.'

Meehan's face was purple with rage and he turned to the barman in fury. 'Get him out of here!'

Harry lifted the bar flap and moved out. 'Right, on your way, mate.'

'I'll go when I'm ready,' Father da Costa told him.

Harry's right hand fastened on his collar, the other on his belt and they went through the door on the run to a chorus of laughter from Donner and Rupert. They crowded to the door to see the fun and Meehan joined them.

Father da Costa was on his hands and knees in the rain in a puddle of water. 'What's up, ducky?' Rupert called. 'Have you pissed yourself or something?'

It was a stupid remark, childish in its vulgarity, and yet it was some sort of final straw that set black rage boiling inside Father da Costa so that when Harry dragged him to his feet, an arm about his throat, he reacted as he had been taught to react thirty years earlier in that hard, brutal school of guerrilla warfare and action by night.

Harry was grinning widely. 'We don't like fancy sods like you coming round here annoying the customers.'

He didn't get a chance to say anything else. Father da Costa's right elbow swung back into his ribs and he pivoted on one foot as Harry reeled back, gasping.

'You should never let anyone get that close. They haven't been teaching you properly.'

Harry sprang forward, his right first swinging in a tremendous punch. Father da Costa swayed to one side, grabbed for the wrist with both hands, twisted it round and up, locking the arm and ran him headfirst into the stack of packing cases.

As Father da Costa turned, Donner came in fast and received a kick under the right kneecap, perfectly delivered, that doubled him over in pain and Father da Costa followed with a knee in the face that lifted him back against the wall.

Rupert gave a cry of dismay and in his haste to regain the safety of the snug, slipped on the top step, bringing Meehan down with him. As Meehan started to get up, Father da Costa punched him in the face, a good, solid right hand that carried all his rage, all his frustration with it. Bone crunched, Meehan's nose flattened beneath Father da Costa's knuckles and he fell back into the snug with a groan, blood gushing from his nostrils.

Rupert scrambled behind the bar on his hands and knees and Father da Costa stood over Meehan, the killing rage still on him, his fists clenched. And then he looked down at his hands, saw the blood on them and an expression of horror appeared on his face.

He backed slowly out into the yard, Harry lay on his face amongst the packing cases, Donner was being sick against the wall. Father da Costa looked in horror once again at the blood on his hands, turned and fled.

When he went into his study at the presbytery, Anna was sitting by the fire knitting. She turned her face towards him. 'You're late. I was worried.'

He was still extremely agitated and had to force himself to sound calm. 'I'm sorry. Something came up.'

She put down her knitting and stood up. 'After you'd gone, when I went down to the church to get ready for choir practice, Fallon was playing the organ.'

He frowned. 'Did he say anything? Did you speak with him?'

'He gave me a message for you,' she told him. 'He said to tell you that it had all been his fault and he was sorry.'

'Was there anything else?'

'Yes, he said that there was no need to worry from now on. That he'd started it, so he'd finish it. And he told me we wouldn't be seeing him again. What did he mean? Do you think he intends to give himself up?'

'God knows,' Father da Costa forced a smile and put a hand on her shoulder, a gesture of reassurance. 'I'm just going down to the church. Something I have to do. I won't be long.'

He left her there and hurried down through the cemetery, entering the church by way of the sacristy. He dropped on his knees at the altar rail, hands clenched together and looked up at Christ on the cross.

'Forgive me,' he pleaded. 'Heavenly Father, forgive me.'

He bowed his head and wept, for in his heart, he knew there was not one single particle of regret for what he had done to Jack Meehan. Worse than that, much worse, was the still, small voice that kept telling him that by wiping Meehan off the face of the earth he would be doing mankind a favour.

Meehan came out of the bathroom at the penthouse wearing a silk kimono and holding an ice-bag to his face. The doctor had been and gone, the bleeding had stopped, but his nose was an ugly, swollen, bruised hump of flesh that would never look the same again. Donner, Bonati and Rupert waited dutifully by the door. Donner's mouth was badly bruised and his lower lip was twice its usual size.

Meehan tossed the ice-bag across the room.

'No bloody good at all, that thing. Somebody get me a drink.'

Rupert hurried to the drinks trolley and poured a large brandy. He carried it across to Meehan who was standing at the window, staring out in the square, frowning slightly.

He turned, suddenly and mysteriously his old self again.

He said to Donner, 'Frank, what was the name of that old kid who was so good with explosives?'

'Ellerman, Mr Meehan, is he the one you're thinking of?'

'That's him. He isn't inside, is he?'

'Not that I know of.'

'Good, then I want him here within the next hour. You go get him and you can tell him there's a couple of centuries in it for him.'

He swallowed some more of his brandy and turned to Rupert. 'And you, sweetheart – I've got just the job for you. You can go and see Jenny for me. We're going to need her, too, for what I have in mind.'

Rupert said, 'Do you think she'll play? She

can be an awkward bitch, when she feels like it.'

'Not this time.' Meehan chuckled. 'I'll give you a proposition to put to her that she can't refuse.'

He laughed again as if it was a particularly good joke and Rupert glanced uncertainly at Donner. Donner said carefully, 'What's it all about, Mr Meehan?'

'I've had enough,' Meehan said. 'That's what it's all about. The priest, Fallon, the whole bit. I'm going to clean the slate once and for all. Take them both out this very night and here's how we're going to do it.'

Harvey Ellerman was fifty years of age and looked ten years older, which came of having spent twenty-two years of his life behind bars if he added his various sentences together.

He was a small diffident individual who habitually wore a tweed cap and brown raincoat and seemed crushed by life, yet this small, anxious-looking man was reputed to know more about explosives than any man in the north of England. In the end, his own genius had proved his undoing, for such was the uniqueness of his approach to the task in hand that it was as if he had signed his own name each time he did a job, and for some years the police had arrested him with monotonous regularity the moment he put a foot wrong.

He came out of the lift into the penthouse, followed by Donner, holding a cheap fibre suitcase in one hand that was bound together by a cheap leather strap. Meehan went to meet him, hand extended, and Ellerman put the suitcase down.

'Great to see you, Harvey,' Meehan said. 'Hope you'll be able to help. Did Frank explain what I'm after?'

'He did, Mr Meehan, in a manner of speaking.' Ellerman hesitated. 'You won't want me personally on this thing, Mr Meehan? There's no question of that?'

'Of course not,' Meehan told him.

Ellerman looked relieved. 'It's just that I've retired from active participation in anything, Mr Meehan,' he said. 'You know how it is?'

'Too true, I do, Harvey. You were too bloody good for them.' He picked up Ellerman's suitcase and put it down on the table. 'Okay, let's see what you've got.'

Ellerman unfastened the strap and opened the suitcase. It contained a varied assortment of explosives carefully packed in tins, a selection of fuses and detonators, neat coils of wire and a rack of tools.

'Frank told me you wanted something similar to the sort of thing the IRA have been using in Ireland.'

'Not just similar, Harvey. I want it to be exactly the same. When the forensic boys get to examine what's left of this bomb I don't want there to be the slightest doubt in their minds where it's come from.'

'All right, Mr Meehan,' Ellerman said in his flat, colourless voice. 'Just as you say.' He produced a tin from the case. 'We'll use this, then. A Waverley biscuit tin. Made in Belfast. Packed with plastic gelignite. Say twenty pounds. That should do the trick.'

'What about a fuse?'

Ellerman held up a long, slim, dark pencil.

'They've been using a lot of these things lately. Chemical fuse of Russian manufacture. Virtually foolproof. Once you break the cap seal you've got twenty minutes.'

'Just the job,' Meehan rubbed his hands together. You'd better get started, then.'

He turned and walked across to the window, whistling happily.

14

Grimsdyke

Fallon came awake to find Jenny shaking him by the shoulder. 'Wake up!' she kept saying insistently. 'Wake up!'

There was a slight persistent throbbing ache behind his right eye, but otherwise he felt strangely light-headed. He sat up, swinging his legs to the floor, and ran his hands over his stubbled chin.

'What time is it?' he asked her.

'About four. Your friend, Father da Costa, was on the phone. He wants to see you.'

Fallon straightened slowly and looked at her, a slight, puzzled frown on his face. 'When was this?'

'About ten minutes ago. I wanted to come and get you, but he said there wasn't time.'

'And where does he want to see me? At Holy Name?'

She shook her head. 'No, he said he was taking his niece into the country. He thought it would be safer for her. A little place called Grimsdyke. It's about twenty miles from here in the marshes. He wants you to meet him there as soon as possible.'

'I see,' Fallon said. 'Do you know where this place is?'

She nodded. 'I used to go there for picnics when I was a kid. I've never been to this place he's going to, Mill House, he called it, but he told me how to get there.'

Fallon nodded slowly. 'And you'd take me?'

'If you like. We could go in my car. It wouldn't take much more than half an hour.'

He stared at her, the eyes very dark, no expression there at all. She glanced away nervously, unable to meet his gaze, and flushed angrily. 'Look, it's no skin of my nose. Do you want to go or don't you?'

He knew she was lying, yet it didn't seem

to matter because for some strange reason he knew beyond any shadow of a doubt that she was leading him in the right direction.

'All right,' he said. 'Fine. Just give me a couple of minutes to get cleaned up. I'll meet you downstairs.'

As soon as she had gone he took the Ceska from his jacket pocket, ejected the magazine, reloaded carefully with eight rounds and slipped it into the right-hand pocket of his trench-coat.

He moved across to the window, dropped to one knee and raised the carpet to disclose a Browning automatic he had used at his first meeting with Kristou in London. Underneath it was a large buff envelope containing the best part of two thousand pounds in ten-pound notes, the bulk of the money he had received from Meehan. He slipped the envelope into his breast pocket and checked the Browning quickly.

He found a roll of surgical tape in the cabinet over the washbasin and cut off a couple of lengths, using the razor Jenny had loaned him, then taped the Browning to the inside of his left leg just above the anklebone, covering it with his sock.

He buttoned his trenchcoat as he went downstairs. Jenny was waiting in the hall dressed in a red plastic mac. She gave him a tight smile as she pulled on her gloves. 'Ready to go, then?'

He opened the front door, but stopped her with a hand on her shoulder as she was about to step outside. 'There isn't anything else, is there? Anything you've forgotten to tell me?'

She flushed and the anger was there in her voice again. 'Would I be likely to do a thing like that?'

'That's all right, then,' He smiled calmly. 'We'd better get going.'

He closed the door and followed her down the steps to the Mini-Cooper parked at the bottom. The marsh at Grimsdyke on the river estuary was a wild, lonely place of sea-creeks and mud flats and great, pale barriers of reeds higher than a man's head. Since the beginning of history men had come here for one purpose or another, Roman, Saxon, Dane, Norman, but now it was a place of ghosts.

An alien world inhabited mainly by the birds, curlew and redshank and brent geese coming south from Siberia for the winter on the mud flats.

They passed through the village, a pleasant enough little place. Thirty or forty houses, a garage and pub, and then they were out on the other side. It was raining quite hard, the wind driving it in off the sea and across the marshes in great clouds.

'Half a mile beyond the village on the right.' Jenny glanced at Fallon briefly. 'That's what the man said.'

'This looks like it,' Fallon told her.

She turned the Cooper off the main road and followed a track no wider than a farm cart that was little more than a raised causeway of grass. On either side miles of rough marsh grass and reeds marched into the heavy rain and a thin sea mist was drifting before the wind.

Fallon lowered the window on his side and took a deep breath of the pungent salt air. 'Quite a place.'

'I used to love coming here when I was a

kid,' she said. 'It was like nowhere else on earth. A different world after the city.'

The closer they got to the estuary, the more the mist seemed to close in on them and then they topped a rise and saw what was very obviously the mill sticking up above a clump of trees about a hundred yards to the south of them.

Fallon put a hand on her arm and she braked to a halt. 'Now what?'

'We'll walk from here.'

'Is that necessary?'

'If I've learned anything in life it's never to take anything for granted.'

She shrugged, but got out of the car without further argument and Fallon left the track and forced his way through a fir plantation towards the mill, dimly seen through the trees.

He crouched under a bush, pulling Jenny down beside him and examined the place carefully. There was a three-storeyed stone tower, roof open to the sky. At one end there was an extension made of wood which looked like a barn and seemed to be in a better state of repair than the rest of the building. A thin trickle of smoke drifted up from an iron chimney.

At the other side there was an immense water-wheel and it was moving round now with an unearthly creaking and groaning, forced by the rushing waters of the flooded stream.

'No sign of his mini-van,' Fallon said softly.

'He'll have it inside that barn, won't he?' Jenny replied, and then added impatiently, 'For goodness sake, make your mind up. Are we going on or aren't we? I'm getting wet.'

She seemed angry and yet the fingers of her left hand trembled slightly. He said, 'You go. Give me a call if everything is all right.'

She glanced at him with a certain surprise in her eyes, then shrugged, stood up and walked out into the open. He watched her go, all the way to the barn. She turned to look at him once, then opened the big double door and went in.

She reappeared a moment later and called, 'It's all right. Everything's fine. Come on.'

Fallon hesitated for a moment and then

shrugged and walked out into the clearing, a slight, fixed smile on his face. When he was four or five yards from the door, Jenny said, 'They're here,' and she went back inside.

He followed her in without hesitation. The place smelled of old hay and mice. There was a decrepit cart in one corner and a large loft ran round three sides of the building with round glassless windows letting in light. A fire was burning in an old iron stove in the corner.

There was no sign of Father da Costa or Anna, not that Fallon had really expected there to be. Only Jenny, standing alone beside a small iron cot bed against the far wall on which a little fair-haired girl was apparently sleeping, covered by a blanket.

'I'm sorry, Martin,' she said, and there was genuine distress in her face now. 'I didn't have any choice.'

'Up here Fallon,' a voice called.

Fallon looked up and saw Donner on the edge of the loft holding an Armalite rifle. Rupert was standing beside him clutching a sawn-off shotgun and Harry, the barman from the Bull and Bell, appeared in the loft at the other side of the building, some sort of revolver in his hand.

Donner raised the Armalite a little. 'They tell me that a bullet from one of these things goes in at the front and out at the back and takes a sizeable piece of you with it on the way, so I'd advise you to stay very still.'

'Oh, I will,' Fallon assured him without irony. And he raised his hands.

Harry came down the ladder from the loft first. He looked terrible. His left eye was completely closed and one side of his face was very badly bruised. He stood a yard or two away, covering Fallon with his revolver while Rupert followed him down the ladder. When they were both in position, Donner lowered the Armalite and joined them.

'Never trust a woman, ducky,' Rupert said with a mocking smile. 'I'd have thought you'd have learnt that. Unreliable bitches, the lot of them. Ruled by the moon. Now me, for instance . . .'

Donner kicked him in the leg. 'Shut up and search him. He'll probably have the shooter in his right-hand pocket.'

Rupert found the Ceska at once and the buff envelope containing the money. Donner looked inside and whistled softly. 'How much?' he demanded.

'Two thousand,' Fallon said.

Donner grinned. 'That must be what they meant by an unexpected bonus.'

He put the envelope in his inside pocket and Rupert started to run his hands over Fallon's body. 'Lovely,' he breathed. 'I could really go for you, ducky,' and he patted Falloc's cheek.

Fallon sent him staggering back with a stiff right arm. 'Put a hand on me again, and I'll break your neck.'

Rupert's eyes glittered and he picked up the sawn-off shotgun and thumbed back the hammer. 'My, my, aren't we butch?' he said softly. 'But I can soon fix that.'

Donner kicked him in the backside. 'You bloody stupid little bitch,' he cried. 'What are you trying to do? Ruin everything at this stage?' He shoved him violently away. 'Go on and make some tea. It's all you're fit for.'

Rupert moved over to the stove sullenly, still clutching his shotgun, and Donner took a pair of regulation police hand-cuffs from his pocket. He snapped them around Fallon's wrists, locked them and slipped the key into his breast pocket.

'You can have it the hard way or you can have it easy,' he said. 'It's all one to me. Understand?'

'I always try to,' Fallon said.

'Right, go and sit down by the bird where I can keep an eye on both of you.'

Fallon moved across to the cot and sat down beside it, his back against the wall. He looked at the child. Her eyes were closed, the breathing easy.

'The daughter you told me about?' he said. 'Is she all right?'

She nodded. 'They gave her a sedative, that's all.' Her eyes were bright with tears. 'I'm sorry, Martin, I didn't have any choice. I collected her after lunch like I do every Saturday and took her to the playground in the local park. That's where Rupert and that creep Harry picked us up.'

'And they threatened you?'

'They said they'd hang on to Sally. That I could have her back if I managed to get you out here.' She put a hand on his arm. 'What else could I do? I was terrified. You don't know Jack Meehan like I do. He's capable of anything – just like Billy.'

'Billy will never bother you again,' Fallon said. 'I killed him last night.'

She stared at him, eyes wide. 'You what?'

'Just as I intend to kill Dandy Jack,' Fallon said calmly. 'There's a packet of cigarettes in my left-hand jacket pocket, by the way. Light me one, will you, like a good girl?'

She seemed stunned by the enormity of what he had said but did as she was told. She put a cigarette in his mouth and as she struck a match, Donner joined them. He was carrying a tartan bag in one hand and squatted down in front of Fallon and unzipped it. One by one he produced three bottles of Irish Whiskey and placed them on the ground.

'Jameson,' Fallon said. 'My favourite. How did you guess?'

'And all for you,' Donner told him. 'All three bottles.'

'I must say it sounds like an interesting idea,' Fallon said. 'Tell me more.'

'Why not?' Donner said. 'Actually, it's very good. I think you'll like it. You see, we have three problems, Fallon. The priest and his niece, because they know more than what's good for them.'

'And me?' Fallon said.

'Exactly.' Donner helped himself to a cigarette. 'Anyway, Mr Meehan had this rather nice idea. It's beautifully simple. We get rid of da Costa and his niece and put the blame on you.'

'I see,' said Fallon. 'And just how do you propose to do that?'

'You were a big man with a bomb in your hand over there in Ulster, weren't you? So it would make sense if you used the same method when you wanted to knock someone off over here.'

'My God,' Jenny said.

327

Donner ignored her and he was obviously enjoying himself. He said, 'Evening Mass at Holy Name is at six o'clock. When it's over, Mr Meehan and Bonati will pick up Father da Costa and his niece and take 'em up that tower, together with about twenty pounds of plastic gelignite and a chemical fuse packed in a Waverley biscuit tin. When that little lot goes up, they go with it and the church comes down.'

'I see,' Fallon said. 'And me – what about me?'

'That's easy. Bonati drives out here in da Costa's mini-van. You get three bottles of Irish Whiskey poured down your throat, we put you behind the wheel and send you for a drive. There's a hill called Cullen's Bend about three miles from here. A terrible place for accidents.'

'And you think that will wrap things up?' Fallon asked him.

'As neat as a Christmas parcel. When they check what's left of that van they'll find bomb-making equipment and a few sticks of gelignite from the same batch the church bomb was manufactured from, not to mention the gun that was used to kill Krasko. The forensic boys will have a field day and let's face it – the Special Branch and Intelligence have been after you for years. They'll be delighted.'

'Miller won't buy it for a second,' Fallon said. 'He knows Meehan was behind the Krasko killing.'

'Perhaps he does, but there won't be a thing he can do about it.'

Jenny said in a whisper, 'It's murder. Cold-blooded murder. You can't do it.'

'Shut your mouth!' Donner said.

She backed away fearfully and then she noticed an extra-ordinary thing. Fallon's eyes seemed to have changed colour slightly, the dark flecked with light, and when he looked up at her there was a power in him that was almost physical, a new authority. Somehow it was as if he had been asleep and was now awake. He glanced across at the other two. Harry was examining the old cart, his back to them, and Rupert stood beside the stove fingering the shotgun.

'That's it then?' he said softly.

Donner shook his head in mock sorrow. 'You should have stayed back home in the bogs, Fallon. You're out of your league.'

'So it would appear,' Fallon said.

Donner leaned across to help himself to another cigarette. Fallon got both hands to the butt of the Browning he had taped so carefully to the inside of his leg above the ankle, tore it free and shot Donner through the heart at point blank range.

The force of the shot lifted Donner off his feet, slamming him back against the ground, and in the same instant Fallon shot Harry in the back before he could turn, the bullet shattering his spine, driving him head first into the cart.

And as Jenny screamed, Fallon knocked her sideways, on his feet now, the Browning arcing towards Rupert as he turned in alarm, already too late, still clutching the shotgun in both hands.

His mouth opened in a soundless scream as Fallon's third bullet caught him squarely in the forehead. Blood and brains sprayed across the grey stones as the skull disintegrated and Rupert was knocked back against the wall, his finger tightening convulsively on the trigger of the shotgun in death, discharging both barrels.

Jenny sprawled protectingly across the child, still deep in her drugged sleep. There was silence. She looked up fearfully and saw that Fallon was standing quite still, legs apart, perfectly balanced, the Browning held out in front of him in both hands. His face was very white, wiped clean of all expression, the eyes dark.

His right sleeve was torn and blood dripped to the floor. She got to her feet unsteadily. 'You're hurt.'

He didn't seem to hear her, but walked to the cart where Harry sprawled on his face and stirred him with his foot. Then he crossed to Rupert.

Jenny moved to join him. 'Is he dead?' she whispered, and then she saw the back of the skull and turned away, stomach heaving, clutching at the wall to steady herself.

When she turned again, Fallon was on his knees beside Donner, fumbling in the dead

331

man's breast pocket. He found the key he was looking for and stood up.

'Get me out of these things.'

The stench of that butcher's shop filled her nostrils, seeped into her very brain, and when she walked towards him, dazed and frightened, she stumbled and almost fell down.

He grabbed her by one arm and held her up. 'Steady, girl. Don't let go now. I need you.'

'I'm fine,' she said. 'Really I am.'

She unlocked the handcuffs. Fallon threw them to one side, dropped to one knee again and took the buff envelope from Donner's inside pocket.

As he stood up, Jenny said wearily, 'You'd better let me have a look at that arm.'

'All right,' Fallon said.

He took off his jacket and sat on the edge of the bed, smoking a cigarette while she did what she could for him.

The arm was a mess. Three of four nasty wounds where steel buckshot had ripped into the flesh. She bandaged it as best she could, with the handkerchief from Donner's breast pocket. Fallon picked up one of the bottles of Jameson, pulled the cork with his teeth and took a long swallow.

When she was finished, she sat on the bed beside him and looked around the barn. 'How long did it take? Two – maybe three seconds?' She shivered. 'What kind of man are you, Martin?'

Fallon pulled on his jacket awkwardly, 'You heard Donner, didn't you? A little Mick out of his league, who should have stayed back home in the bogs.'

'He was wrong, wasn't he?'

'Where I come from, he wouldn't have lasted a day,' Fallon said dispassionately. 'What time is it?'

She glanced at her watch. 'Five-thirty.'

'Good.' He stood up and reached for his trenchcoat. 'Evening Mass at Holy Name starts at six and finishes around seven. You take me there – now.'

She helped him on with the trenchcoat. 'That boat,' she said. 'The one you were supposed to leave on from Hull? I heard the name. Donner and Rupert were talking. You could still go.'

'Without a passport?'

He turned, trying to belt his coat, awkwardly because of his wounded arm, and she did it for him.

'Money talks,' she said. 'And you've got plenty in that envelope.'

She stood very close, her hands around his waist, looking up at him. Fallon said calmly, 'And you'd like to come with me, I suppose?'

She shook her head. 'You couldn't be more wrong. It's too late for me to change now. It was too late the day I started. It's you I'm thinking of. You're the only man I've ever known who gave me more than a quick tumble and the back of his hand.'

Fallon stared at her somberly for a long moment and then said quietly, 'Bring the child.'

He walked to the door. Jenny picked up her daughter, wrapped her in a blanket and followed. When she went outside, he was standing, hands in pockets, staring up into the rain where brent geese passed overhead in a V formation.

He said quietly, 'They're free and I'm not, Jenny. Can you understand that?'

334

When he took his right hand out of his pocket, blood dripped from the fingers. She said, 'You need a doctor.'

'I need Dandy Jack Meehan and no one else,' he said. 'Now let's get out of here.' And he turned and led the way back along the track to the car.

15

The Wrath of God

Meehan was feeling pleased with himself, in spite of his broken nose, as he and Bonati walked past the town hall. Pleased and excited. His Homburg was set at a jaunty angle, the collar of his double-breasted melton overcoat was turned up against the wind, and he carried a canvas holdall containing the bomb in his right hand.

'I know one thing,' he said to Bonati as they crossed the road. 'I'd like to know where our Billy is right now. I'll have the backside off him for this when I see him.'

'You know what it's like for these young lads when they get with a bird, Mr Meehan,' Bonati said soothingly. 'He'll turn up.'

'Bloody little tarts,' Meehan said in disgust. 'All that lad ever thinks of is his cock-end.'

He turned the corner into Rockingham Street and received his first shock when he heard the organ playing at Holy Name and voices raised in song.

He dodged into a doorway out of the rain and said to Bonati, 'What in the hell goes on here? Evening Mass starts at six. I only make it ten to.'

'Search me, Mr Meehan.'

They crossed the street, heads down in a flurry of rain, and paused at the notice board. Bonati peered up, reading it aloud. 'Evening Mass, six o'clock, Saturdays, five-thirty.'

Meehan swore softly. 'A bloody good job we were early. Come on, let's get inside.'

It was cold in the church and damp and the smell of the candles was very distinctive. There were only a dozen people in the congregation. Father da Costa was up at the altar praying and on the other side of the green baize curtain, Meehan could see Anna da Costa's head as she played the organ.

He and Bonati sat down at one side, partially hidden by a pillar, and he put the canvas holdall between his feet. It was really quite pleasant sitting there in the half-darkness, Meehan decided, with the candles flickering and the organ playing. The four acolytes in their scarlet cassocks and white cottas reminded him nostalgically of his youth. Strangest thing of all, he found that he could remember some of the responses.

'I confess to Almighty God, and to you, my brothers and sisters,' said Father da Costa, 'that I have sinned through my own fault.'

He struck his breast and Meehan joined in enthusiastically, asking blessed Mary ever Virgin, all the angels and saints and the rest of the congregation to pray for him to the Lord our God.

As they all stood for the next hymn it suddenly struck him, with something like surprise, that he was thoroughly enjoying himself.

* * *

As the Cooper went over a humped-back bridge, Fallon, who had been sitting with his head forward on his chest, sat up with a start.

'Are you all right?' Jenny asked him anxiously.

'I'm fine,' he said and his voice was calm and perfectly controlled.

He touched his right arm gingerly. The shock effects were wearing off now and it was beginning to hurt like hell. He winced and Jenny noticed at once.

'I think I should take you straight to the Infirmary.'

He ignored the remark and turned to look at the child who lay on the back seat, still in her drugged sleep, wrapped in the blanket in which Jenny had carried from the mill.

'She's a nice kid,' he said.

The road was dangerous now in the heavy rain as darkness fell and needed all her attention, yet there was something in his voice that caused her to glance warily at him.

He lit a cigarette one-handed and leaned back against the seat. 'I'd like you to know something,' he said. 'What Donner said back there about me being bomb-happy wasn't true. Those kids in that school bus – it was an accident. They walked into an ambush we'd laid for a Saracen armoured car. It was a mistake.'

He hammered his clenched fist against his right knee in a kind of frenzy.

'I know,' Jenny told him. 'I understand.'

'That's good, that's marvellous,' he said. 'Because I never have.'

The agony in his voice was more than she could bear and she concentrated on the road, tears in her eyes.

As the congregation moved out, Anna continued to play and Father da Costa went into the sacristy with the acolytes. He took off his cope as the boys got out of their cassocks and into their street clothes. He saw them out of the side door, bidding each one of them good night.

Anna was still playing, something more powerful now, which meant that the last of the congregation had left. She always seemed to sense that moment. It was Bach again from the sound of it. The piece Fallon had played. She stopped abruptly. Father da Costa paused in the act of pulling off his alb and waited, but she did not start playing again. He frowned, opened the sacristy door and went into the church.

Anna was standing at the altar rail and Jack Meehan was holding her firmly by the arm. Father da Costa took an angry step forward and Bonati moved from behind a pillar holding a Luger in his left hand.

It stopped Father da Costa dead in his tracks and Meehan smiled. 'That's better. Now we're all going to take a little ride in the cage up to the catwalk. There's only room for two at a time so we'll have to split up. I'll stick with the girl, you go with Bonati, Father, and remember one thing. Anything you try that's the slightest bit out of turn will be reflected in the girl's treatment, so keep your hands to yourself and don't try any rough stuff.'

'All right, Mr Meehan,' Father da Costa said. 'What do you want with me?'

'All in good time.' Meehan pushed Anna across to the hoist, opened the cage door and followed her inside. As they started to rise he looked out at Father da Costa. 'Remember what I told you,' he said. 'So don't try anything funny.'

Father da Costa waited, the black, killing rage in him again and he fought to control it. What on earth did the man want? What was it all about? When the hoist descended again, he rushed inside eagerly and Bonati followed him and pressed the button.

When it jolted to a halt, Father da Costa opened the gate at once and stepped out. Meehan had switched the light on and the boards of the catwalk, wet with rain, glistened in the darkness.

Anna was standing, one hand on the rail, complete uncertainty on her face. Father da Costa took a step towards her and Meehan produced a Browning from his pocket. 'Stay where you are!' He nodded to Bonati. 'Tie his wrists together.'

There was little that Father da Costa could

do except comply and he put his arms behind him. Bonati lashed his wrists together quickly with a piece of thin twine.

'Now the girl,' Meehan said.

Anna didn't say a word as Bonati repeated the performance. As he finished, her uncle moved to join her. 'Are you all right?' he asked her in a low voice.

'I think so,' she said. 'What's going to happen to us?'

'I'm afraid you'll have to address that question to Mr Meehan personally,' he said. 'I'm sure I don't know.'

Meehan unzipped the holdall, slipped his hand inside and broke the detonating cap on the chemical fuse, then he zipped the bag up again and put it down casually at the side of the catwalk in the shadows.

'All right, Father, I'll tell you what I'm going to do with you. I'm going to leave you and your niece up here on your own for fifteen minutes to meditate. When I return, I hope to find you in a more reasonable frame of mind. If not, then . . .'

'But I don't understand,' Father da Costa interrupted. 'What on earth are you hoping to accomplish?'

At that moment, the organ in the church below broke into the opening bars of the Bach Prelude and Fugue in D major.

The astonishment on Meehan's face was something to see. 'It's Fallon,' he whispered.

'It can't be,' Bonati said.

'Then who the hell am I listening to – a ghost playing?' Meehan's anger overflowed like white-hot lava. 'Go and get him,' he raved. 'Bring the bastard up here. Tell him the girl gets it if he doesn't come.'

Bonati hurriedly stepped into the cage, closed the gate and started down. When he was halfway there, the organ stopped playing. The cage juddered to a halt. It was suddenly very quiet. He cocked the Luger, kicked the gate open and stepped out.

When the Cooper turned into Rockingam Street and pulled up opposite Holy Name, Fallon was leaning in the corner, eyes-closed.

At first Jenny thought he was unconscious, or, at the very least, asleep, but when she touched him gently he opened his eyes at once and smiled at her.

'Where are we?'

'Holy Name,' she said.

He took a deep breath and straightened up. 'Good girl.' He put a hand inside his coat and produced the buff envelope and passed it across to her. 'There's nearly two thousand pounds in there. The money I received from Jack Meehan on account and hard earned. I won't need it where I'm going. Go off somewhere. Somewhere you've never even heard of. Take the kid with you and try again.'

The envelope was slippery with blood as she examined it in the light from the instrument panel. 'Oh my God,' she said, and then she switched on the interior light and turned to look at him. 'Oh, Martin,' she said in horror. 'There's blood all over you.'

'It doesn't matter,' he said, and he opened the car door.

She got out on her side. 'He'll kill you,' she said desperately. 'You don't know him like I do. You don't stand a chance. Let me get the police. Let Mr Miller handle him.'

'God save us, but I've never asked a policeman for help in my life.' A slight, ironic smile touched Fallon's mouth fleetingly. 'Too late to start now.' He patted her face gently. 'You're a nice girl, Jenny. A lovely girl. It didn't touch you, any of it. Always believe that. Now get the hell out of it and God bless you.'

He turned and crossed the road to Holy Name. Jenny got into the Cooper and started the engine. He was going to his death, she was convinced of that, and the compulsion to save him was something that she was unable to deny.

Suddenly resolute, she drove round the corner, stopped at the first telephone-box she came to and dialled nine-nine-nine. When they put her through to the main switchboard at police headquarters, she asked for Detective-Superintendent Miller.

There were still lights at the windows, but it was the absence of music that Fallon found puzzling until, gazing up at the noticeboard, he made the same discovery that Jack Meehan had about the time of evening Mass on a Saturday.

Panic moved inside him. Oh my God, he thought. I'm too late.

The door went back against the wall with a crash that echoed throughout the silent building, but the church was empty. Only the eternal ruby light of the sanctuary lamp, the flickering candles, the Virgin smiling sadly down at him, Christ high on his cross down there by the altar.

He ran along the centre aisle and reached the hoist. The cage was not there. They were still on top and he was conscious of a fierce joy. He pressed the button to bring the cage down, but nothing happened. He pressed it again with the same result. *Which meant that the cage was standing open up there.*

He hammered his clenched fist against the wall in despair. There had to be a way to bring Meehan down. There had to be.

And there was, of course, and it was so

beautifully simple that he laughed out loud, his voice echoing up the nave as he turned and moved towards the altar rail and went up through the choir stalls.

He sat down on the organ stool, switched on and pulled out an assortment of stops feverishly. There was blood on the keys, but that didn't matter and he moved into the opening of the Bach Prelude in D Major. The glorious music echoed between the walls as he gave it everything he had, ignoring the pain in his right hand and arm.

'Come on, you bastard!' he shouted aloud. 'Let's be having you.'

He stopped playing and was immediately aware of the slight clanging the cage made on its descent. He got up and went down the steps through the choir stalls, drawing the Ceska from his pocket and screwing the silencer into place with difficulty, arriving at the correct vantage point as the cage reached ground level.

Fallon flattened himself against the wall and waited, the Ceska ready. The cage door was kicked open and Bonati stepped out, clutching the Luger. Fallon shot him through the hand and Bonati dropped the Luger with a sharp cry and turned to face him.

'Meehan,' Fallon said. 'Is he up there?'

Bonati was shaking like a leaf in a storm, frightened out of his wits. He tried to speak, but could only manage to nod his head vigorously.

'All right.' Fallon smiled and Bonati saw that face again, a face to frighten the Devil. 'Go home and change your ways.'

Bonati needed no second bidding and ran up the aisle clutching his wrist. The door banged behind him, the candles fluttered. It was quiet again. Fallon moved into the cage and pressed the button to ascend.

On the catwalk, Meehan, Anna and Father da Costa waited, the rain falling in silver strands through the yellow light. The cage jerked to a halt, the door swung open. It was dark in there.

Meehan raised his Browning slightly. 'Bonati?'

Fallon drifted out of the darkness, a pale ghost. 'Hello, you bastard,' he said.

Meehan started to take aim and Father da Costa ducked low in spite of his bound hands and shouldered him to the rail, tripping him deftly so that Meehan fell heavily. The Browning skidded along the catwalk and Fallon kicked it into space.

He leaned against the rail for support, suddenly strangely tired, his arm really hurting now, and gestured with the Ceska.

'All right, untie him.'

Meehan did as he was told reluctantly and the moment he was free, Father da Costa untied Anna. He turned to Fallon, concern in his voice. 'Are you all right?'

Fallon kept all his attention on Meehan. 'The bomb? Have you set the fuse?'

'Get stuffed,' Meehan told him.

'Bomb?' Father da Costa demanded.

'Yes,' Fallon said. 'Did he have a bag with him?'

'Over there,' Father da Costa pointed to where the canvas holdall stood in the shadows.

'All right,' Fallon said, 'You'd better get Anna out of here fast and I mean out. If that thing goes off it will bring the whole church down like a house of cards.'

Father da Costa didn't even hesitate. He grabbed Anna by the arm and guided her towards the hoist, but she pulled free and turned towards Fallon. 'Martin!' she cried and caught at his trenchcoat. 'We can't go without you.'

'The cage only takes two at a time,' he said. 'Be sensible.'

There was blood on her hand from his sleeve and she held it close to her face as if trying to see it. 'Oh my God,' she whispered.

Father da Costa put an arm around her shoulders and said to Fallon, 'You're hurt.'

'You're running out of time,' Fallon said patiently.

Father da Costa pushed Anna inside the cage and followed her in. As he pressed the button to descend he called through the bars, 'I'll be back, Martin, Wait for me.'

His voice was swallowed up by darkness and Fallon turned to Meehan and smiled,

'You and me, Jack at the final end of things. Isn't that something? We can go to hell together.'

'You're mad,' Meehan said. 'I'm not waiting here to die. I'm going to get rid of this thing.'

He moved towards the holdall and Fallon raised the Ceska threateningly. 'I've had experience, remember? At this stage it'll go up at the slightest touch.' He chuckled. 'I'll tell you what we'll do. We'll leave it with God. If the cage gets back in time, we leave. If not . . .'

'You raving bloody lunatic.' Meehan was shouting now.

Fallon said calmly, 'By the way, I've just remembered I've got something for you.' He produced a crumpled white card with a black border and held it out.

Meehan said, 'What in hell is that supposed to be?'

'A Rest-in-Peace card, isn't that what you call them? It's for Billy. Plot number five hundred and eighty-two at Pine Trees.'

Meehan seemed stunned. 'You're lying.'

Fallon shook his head. 'I killed him last

night because he tried to rape Anna da Costa.
I took him up to the crematorium and put
him through the whole process, just like you
showed me. Last I saw of your brother, he
was five pounds of grey ash scattered across
damp grass.'

Meehan seemed to break into a thousand
pieces. 'Billy!' he screamed and went for
Fallon, head down.

Fallon pulled the trigger of the Ceska.
There was a dull click and then Meehan was
on him, smashing him back against the guard
rail. It splintered, sagged, then gave way and
Fallon went over the edge into space. He hit
the canvas tarpaulin stretched over the hole
in the roof and went straight through.

Meehan turned and reached for the holdall.
As he picked it up and turned to throw it
out into the darkness, it exploded.

As Father da Costa and Anna went out of
the door into the street, two police cars
arrived at speed. Miller scrambled out of the
first one and hurried towards them. As he

put a foot on the first step leading up to the porch, the bomb exploded.

The effect was extraordinary, for the whole church started to fall in, almost in slow motion, first the tower, the steel scaffolding crumpling around it, and then the roof.

Miller grabbed Anna's other arm and he and Father da Costa ran her down into the safety of the street between them. As they reached the cars, a scaffolding pole rebounded from the wall of the warehouse above their heads and everyone ducked.

Father da Costa was first on his feet and stood, fists clenched, gazing up at the church. As the dust cleared, he saw that most of the walls and the rear entrance porch were still standing.

A young constable came forward from one of the police cars holding a spot lamp and Father da Costa simply took it from him and turned to Miller. 'I'm going back in.'

He started forward and Miller grabbed him by the arm. 'You must be crazy.'

'Fallon was in there,' Father da Costa said.

'He saved us, don't you understand? He might still be alive. I must know.'

'Fallon?' Miller said in astonishment. 'My God, so it was Fallon all the time.'

Father da Costa hurried up the steps to the porch and pushed open the door. The scene inside was incredible. Holy Name was finished; at the end of things at last, but the worst damage was by the tower or what was left of it.

Father da Costa went up the central aisle, flashing the spot before him. The area in front of the altar where the tower and roof had come down together was a mountain of bricks and mortar.

The spot picked out something inside. It could have been a face, he wasn't sure. There seemed to be a tunnel of sorts. He got down on his hands and knees and started to crawl through, holding the spot before him.

He found Fallon at the end of the tunnel, only his head and shoulders exposed. The figure of Christ on the cross, the large one which had stood by the altar, had fallen across him protectingly, at least for the moment.

Father da Costa crouched beside him and the great cross sagged under the weight it was holding and dust descended on his head.

'Martin?' he said. 'Can you hear me?'

There was a scraping sound behind him as Miller arrived. 'For God's sake, Father,' he said, 'We must get out of here. The whole damn lot might come down at any moment.'

Father da Costa ignored him. 'Martin?'

Fallon opened his eyes. 'Did you get Anna out?'

'I did, Martin.'

'That's all right, then. I'm sorry. Sorry for everything.'

The cross sagged a little more, stones and rubble cascaded over Father da Costa's back and he leaned across Fallon to protect him.

'Martin.' he said. 'Can you hear me?' Fallon opened his eyes. 'I want you to make an act of contrition. Say after me: my God, who art infinitely good in Thyself . . .'

'O my God,' Martin Fallon said and died.

There was a long silence. Even that mass of rubble and debris seemed to have stopped moving. For some strange reason Miller suddenly felt as if he didn't belong, as if he had no right to be there. He turned and started to crawl out.

Behind him, Father Michael da Costa got down on his knees, head bowed beneath that frail roof, and started to pray for the soul of the man who had called himself Martin Fallon.

Without Mercy

Jack Higgins

In Jack Higgins' acclaimed bestseller *Dark Justice*, intelligence operative Sean Dillon and his colleagues in Britain and the United States beat back a terrible enemy, but at an equally terrible cost. One of them was shot, another run down in the street. Both were expected to survive – but only one of them does.

As Detective Superintendent Hannah Bernstein of Special Branch lies recuperating in the hospital, a dark shadow from their past, scarred deep by hatred, steals across the room and finishes the job. Consumed by grief and rage, Dillon, Blake, Ferguson and all who loved Hannah swear vengeance, no matter where it takes them. But they have no idea of the searing journey upon which they are about to embark – nor of the war which will change them all.

'Higgins is a master of his craft'   *Daily Telegraph*

ISBN 978-0-00-719945-7